HELLFIRE
IN TRIPOLI

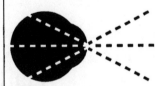

This Large Print Book carries the
Seal of Approval of N.A.V.H.

HELLFIRE
IN TRIPOLI

Edwin P. Hoyt

G.K. Hall & Co. • Thorndike, Maine

Published in 2000 by arrangement with Wieser & Wieser, Inc.

G.K. Hall Large Print Paperback Series.

The text of this Large Print edition is unabridged.
Other aspects of the book may vary from the original edition.

Set in 16 pt. Plantin by Rick Gundberg.

Printed in the United States on permanent paper.

Library of Congress Cataloging-in-Publication Data

Hoyt, Edwin Palmer.
   Hellfire in Tripoli / by Edwin P. Hoyt.
      p. cm.
   ISBN 0-7838-8833-3 (lg. print : sc : alk. paper)
   1. Decatur, Stephen, 1779–1820 — Fiction. 2. United States —
History — Tripolitan War, 1801–1805 — Fiction. 3. United States
— History, Naval — 19th century — Fiction. 4. Admirals — United
States — Fiction. 5. Tripoli — History — Fiction. 6. Large type
books. I. Title.
PS3558.O97 H45 2000
813'.54—dc21
                                                            99-055523

HELLFIRE
IN TRIPOLI

1

Lieutenant Stephen Decatur put down the glass and smiled as he looked across the choppy gray water of the Mediterranean at the long tongue of land and the line of reefs and shoals that jutted out to the east. His wavy brown hair was parted and disarranged by the stiff offshore breeze — he had taken off his heavy triangular cap to see better through the glass at the Tripoli harbor, and although it was a fair seaman's day for the winter of 1804, it was cold and nasty by a landlubber's standards; the men in the fo'c'sle claimed it could knock the peas out of the porridge.

But Lieutenant Decatur, even without his greatcoat, did not notice the cold or the biting wind. The smile that creased the handsome high-browed face with its deep-set eyes and strong nose was there because Stephen Decatur had just decided on a most outrageous enterprise. He would invade that rocky, shallow harbor entrance, and give the Bashaw of Tripoli a lesson in the arts of war that he would not soon forget.

"Steady as she goes," Decatur shouted over his shoulder to the helmsman. It was necessary to shout in the teeth of that Tripolitanian wind. "I want another look at that shoal water."

It was totally unnecessary for the captain of the United States schooner of war *Enterprise* to explain himself to his quartermaster, but that was Decatur's way.

The hundred men of the twelve-gun warship knew more about what was on their captain's mind at any given time than did the seamen of any other ship in the fleet, including Commodore Edward Preble's proud frigate *Constitution.* There had been many a black eye and bloodied head in the harbor at Syracuse, back on the shore of the Two Sicilies, before the tars of the other ships would admit as much. But in the last two months the *Enterprise* had taken on the convincer. Bosun's Mate Abby Tyler from Marblehead, Massachusetts, had come around, and he was the biggest and strongest brawler in the American squadron. Even the commodore's crew now admitted that Lieutenant Decatur knew how to treat a man and had the makings of a great commander. There had not been a flogging aboard the *Enterprise* since he took over command from Isaac Hull, but discipline had never been tighter. The men knew, as much as orders permitted, just where they were going and what they were doing every day, and they turned to with a will that made little *Enterprise* the spit-and-polish ship of the fleet. Even the commodore could have eaten from her gallery deck after morning holystoning. For with a word or a look, Lieutenant Decatur could make a man feel like a hero or a fool. "When he crinkles up them eyes at yer," said Abby Tyler, "ye'll go to Hell for 'im."

"Or if ye've put too much pepper in the gullion, he'll make ye want to jump in yerself," added Cronky Willet, the ship's cook, as the pair huddled over a tot of highly irregular rum to warm their bones in the windy galley that January morning.

Lieutenant Decatur knew of the long-standing friendship of the cook and bosun's mate, and was quite aware of the irregular dispensation of the ship's rum, but he ignored these breaches of Washington's discipline as unimportant as long as the ship ran itself the way he wanted. And this morning, adjusting his twenty-five-year-old legs to the rolling of his little ship, he knew or sensed everything that was going on aboard her, even as his attention was focused on the Tripolitanian shore seven miles away.

The excitement grew. Decatur peered through the glass again, as the helmsman followed orders and tacked the schooner in toward the lee shore, coming back now from the south to get another look at the enemy harbor. Inside, Decatur could see the castellated defenses, and southeast on the shore, Fort English, so named because it had already been built by the English prisoners of war captured by the pirates, who ravaged these seas in search of booty and prisoners who could be ransomed. These Barbary pirates of Tripoli

9

and Algiers had virtually destroyed commerce in the Mediterranean a quarter century earlier and now held it in bondage. Everyone, the United States included, paid tribute to the Bashaw and the Dey of Algiers. The Bashaw, greedier now than in times past, was so restless that he flaunted his power and had a few months earlier taken the prize that now came into Stephen Decatur's focused glass.

There she was, proud and tall as she had been when his father sailed her, the United States frigate *Philadelphia*, held there, moored in the middle of the outer harbor among a handful of rakish pirate craft. Looking carefully, adjusting to the sway and cant of the deck, Decatur saw more through his glass. Last time he had passed this spot, the *Philadelphia*'s yards had been bare, and she was low in the water. Captain William Bainbridge had bored holes in her bottom and torn down her sails and running rigging before scuttling the *Philadelphia* when she had so unfortunately grounded on an uncharted reef while chasing an unlikely looking sail last October. Proud ship, proud captain had both been helpless. The tide departed, leaving the frigate canted over so that her guns could not be brought down from the sky on the one side or up from the deep on the other to point at the little pirate gunboats that came along and threatened to kill the crew off, man by man, snarling around the ship like angry bees. So Bainbridge had made ready to scuttle and then had surrendered her, sure that if the Bashaw's men tried to pull her off, she would sink deep and forever.

But an autumn storm had driven her up high and dry, and the Bashaw's admiral saw that her bottom could be repaired, and did so — then towed her off grandly into Tripoli harbor to be greeted by the huzzahs of the faithful.

The Bashaw had never been so happy. Since the moment when he had learned that his archrival, the Dey of Algiers, had been given an American frigate as a bit of blackmail, he had wanted one of his own, and now he had it.

Through the long brassbound glass, a gift from his father, Captain Stephen Decatur, the young lieutenant saw what had not been there before. The yards had sprouted sail, neatly furled along the length of them. The tops and gallants were in place, the running rigging had been restored, and where the green crescent flag hung, he could see that the *Philadelphia* was being readied for sea. He could imagine the rest — how the Bashaw's sailors had been ordered to learn immediately to man the new kind of vessel, and how within a matter of days, perhaps, she would be out in the broad Mediterranean. The *Enterprise* could not stand up against her forty-four guns, nor could any ship of the squadron, save the *Constitution* herself. That kind of fight, American commodore against American ship turned pirate — could not bring glory to anyone and must redound to the disgrace of the navy, no matter how it ended.

11

Decatur's heart stopped for a moment as he thought of what he might do. He could take the *Enterprise* right this moment, maneuver to fire the twelve-pounders to strike below the water line, and delay the sailing. But around and beyond the *Philadelphia*, as the glass ranged, Decatur could see the lateen-rigged gunboats, which were ready to dart through the gaps in the reef. Not one of them could face the *Enterprise* in a battle at sea — he could take on three or four with ease, he knew. But he counted — twelve, fourteen, sixteen — there were too many of them, and they were too well suited for close work in these confined waters. He *could* do the job today, but . . .

And the but was that he would very likely lose the *Enterprise.* He knew what that would mean — not glory, but at the very least a severe reprimand from the Old Man.

The Old Man, Commodore Preble, was scarcely old at all — in his early forties — but he was a fearsome figure here in the Mediterranean. He had a disposition like a sleepy bear, the courage of a raging lion, and the wit of a philosopher, but above all, the disciplinary sense of a Nelson. Over endless glasses of port in his cabin on the *Constitution*, the Old Man had drummed into Decatur and the other "schoolboy captains" of his little fleet that they must first of all obey his orders. There would be time later for heroism. And, as Decatur explained his actions when he could to the men on the lower deck, the Old

Man had raised the glass to the lantern jaw and the generous mouth, thrown back his grizzled head in that typical gesture, and hunched his lean form forward across the table to expound.

"I'll damn your eyes, young Decatur, if you ever risk the *Enterprise* before I tell you to. Bainbridge wouldn't be where he is right now, looking down through bars at his ship, if the *Vixen* had not been off chasing rainbows that day. The job of a schooner in this squadron is to test the water for old *Connie* and don't you ever forget it. You may have to pull me off a reef one of these days, and I want you there when I need you. Understood?"

There was small chance of avoiding understanding when the Old Man talked that way, and so Stephen Decatur had tightened the bit on his ambition, and now, looking through his glass, he regretfully abandoned the momentary impulse to sail in the teeth of the Berbers and cut the *Philadelphia* down.

As the little schooner moved in toward the shore, Decatur could see the activity increase on deck of the *Philadelphia*. They were loading stores, by God, and that meant it really was just a few days till the ship might be out at sea, challenging the squadron.

He must get back to Syracuse immediately, and pass the word to Commodore Preble. The *Philadelphia* could not be allowed to sail. The damage to American prestige by her capture was nothing compared to what would come of her depredations on the sea; the American navy would become the laughingstock of the world.

Lieutenant Decatur snapped the glass away from his eye and stood straight, issuing his orders.

"Prepare to come about. Mr. Macdonough, tell the first lieutenant I want him. Come on boys. We're going home to Syracuse."

He watched then, as his crew turned to with a will that never failed to please him. If the old adage was "one hand for the ship and one for the man," then the sailors of Decatur's schooner must have three hands, said the others in the squadron, for she was the tautest vessel in Syracuse, and always the quickest to move.

The midshipman, Thomas Macdonough, ran off to find Lieutenant Lawrence, and in five minutes the ship had turned about, and was heading off on a long northwest tack that would pull her close to her destination.

As they left the coast of Tripoli, the sky cleared, and the January sun came forth to warm the men on deck. Decatur, hat clapped securely on his handsome head, moved forward and aft, pacing, watching, smiling, and occasionally nodding to the men as they worked. Without in any way easing discipline or lowering himself, the young captain made his men feel that both he and they were parts of the ship, and that they were as important as he.

Pacing, watching, stopping to chat with his officers, Decatur never failed to notice all that was

14

going on about him. And an hour later, when the forward lookout shouted "Sail ho," and turned, Decatur was already in the shrouds, halfway up the ratlines, that awkward captain's tricorner rolling on the deck, glass in hand, staring out to sea.

The vessel he espied was a ketch, a common enough sight in these waters, with sharp-raked mainmast and long lateen sail, and the queer blunt nose of a Mediterranean hull. She could be a simple trading vessel headed from Malta or even Syracuse. She could also be a pirate ship, headed home to the African shore with booty, for she was moving toward the *Enterprise*, which meant toward Tripoli harbor, if it did not mean a reach for Crete. She was certainly worth investigating — and Lieutenant Decatur was even more certain of it when the ship changed course. Of course, it might mean that the captain had decided to move away, fearing pirates. Or it might mean that he was one.

"Let's take a look," he shouted. "Run her down."

The schooner piled on sail, then the ketch turned straight east to run before the wind and escape across their bows. One tack, and they were reaching northeast on a comfortable run. An hour later, the ketch came suddenly about, tacking desperately back toward the African shore, but the maneuver cost her ten minutes and a mile's distance between them, and although the little ketch moved more freely into

15

the wind, Decatur's seamanship brought the schooner ever closer.

Soon only a mile separated the vessels, and then it was three-quarters of a mile. Through his glass, Decatur saw a flurry of activity aboard the smaller vessel, and then suddenly it all disappeared. Her captain, seeing that she was going to be overhauled, and that she was too far from shore for him to take advantage of the reefs and openings that the small vessel could negotiate so easily, had decided to stop running.

"Hoist the colors," said Decatur. "If she's a trader she'll know she has nothing to fear from us."

The Stars and Stripes went swiftly up the masthead, and as if to respond, the little ketch turned up into the wind, and hung in irons, her mainsail shivering in the breeze.

They approached to two hundred yards, and Decatur could see her decks. Odd, there were only four seamen visible, the captain on the poop, wearing turban and the great loose shirt of the Arab world. The little vessel could be anything, but he could have sworn that an hour ago he had seen at least thirty or forty men along those bulwarks. It was more than a little odd.

"Careful boys," he said, and stepped down out of the rigging. They were within gunshot. No use to take chances.

Midshipman Thomas Macdonough moved forward, hesitantly.

"Well?" the harsh question was accompanied by a smile.

"Please sir, the first lieutenant wants to know should he send a boat?"

"Tell him to wait. We'll go alongside. I wouldn't want to risk a boat or a man's life if this little tub is what I think she is."

"Aye, aye, sir. I'll tell him to wait." The midshipman scurried forward.

Decatur moved close to the helmsman so he could talk quietly.

"Pull her alongside now, Fraser," he said, "just as close as we can come without scraping. Let's see what happens."

He then moved forward, and spoke quietly to the first lieutenant. The men were armed with cutlass, musket, or pistol, and half the crew was stationed below deck, so the other ship's captain might not ascertain their true strength.

As the distance between the vessels decreased, Decatur cupped his hands and hailed.

"What vessel?"

The bearded captain, lounging at the wheel, shrugged and put up his hands.

"Quel vaisseau?"

Another shrug.

Rapidly, Decatur hailed in Italian and Spanish, and then, still receiving no answer, he turned.

"Ready to board, men. Grappling hooks. Into the rigging!"

As these words rang out, the lounging captain

suddenly sprang into action, and shouted in Arabic. From the bowels of the ketch and up from the bulwarks where they had been lying flat on deck, came his crew, some forty howling, yelling Barbary pirates, in turbans and shirts of every hue, pistols in their hands, scimitars clutched tight, and long curved daggers at their waists.

"Give them a volley," shouted Decatur, and the guns of his marines began to fire. He sensed the question of his gun captains. "Hold the guns, we're going to board, I want this one whole."

The screaming, gesticulating Berbers began firing their weapons irregularly, and small cannon on the bow spoke, but the aim was poor, the gun could not be trained, and the shot passed harmlessly off the beam of the schooner.

"Bring her in now, Fraser, slow and easy." Decatur glanced up at the mainsail; they were moving upwind, and in a moment the wind would be blanketed by the ketch. It was now.

"Bring her up." He spoke sharply, and even as Fraser complied, and the *Enterprise* moved to scrape along the side of the lower vessel, Decatur was in motion, leaping across the two-foot spread of open water and calling his men.

"Come on boys! We have them now."

He headed astern to challenge the captain of the Barbary vessel, and as he came up, sword in hand, he cut down one ragged barefoot pirate who jabbed at him with a pike, but did not stop in stride until he reached the wheel.

The Berber captain, snarling and spewing forth a torrent of abuse in Arabic, slashed at him with a scimitar, and leaped nimbly behind the wheel, clawing with his left hand at a long dagger. Across the wheel, Decatur parried the thrust of the curved sword with his cutlass, and reached into his pocket and pulled out his pistol. He fired through the wheel, and the Arab captain fell dead, shot through the heart.

Decatur turned, and saw that behind him, officers and men of the *Enterprise* were acquitting themselves well. Young Macdonough had a scimitar cut on his hand, but his eyes were bright, and he was herding before him two wicked looking Arabs who had suddenly decided they did not wish to fight further. Ten minutes later it was all over, the ketch was carried, and the *Enterprise* had lost only one man killed, and three wounded. A dozen live prisoners were taken aboard the schooner for delivery to the court of the Two Sicilies. Undoubtedly they would be freed in little time, but that was unimportant. For Stephen Decatur had what he wanted, a shoal water vessel, and he had a plan.

2

On the way to the beautiful Sicilian harbor of Syracuse, Lieutenant Decatur began to piece together the story of the vessel he had captured. From reading her papers and questioning the crew, he had learned that the name of the vessel was the *Mastico* and that she had participated in the capture of the *Philadelphia*.

This information caused him to slap his leg as he sat at the tiny desk in his cabin. He could scarcely wait to get to Syracuse to see the Old Man, and put forth the proposal he now had perfected in his mind for the confusion of the enemy.

They sailed into Syracuse harbor on a bright, sunny morning, so warm it was almost hard to believe it was still January. In they came, past the mole, the *Enterprise* leading, the captive ship and its prize crew trailing behind her. Anchored just a few chains from the flagship, Lieutenant Decatur lost no time in getting the gig overboard, his boat crew straining to take him to the *Constitution*. He was piped aboard, for although he was only a lieutenant, he was also captain of a vessel and in this foreign port, the Americans took some pains to show dignity. The British were forever trying to lord it over the former colonials, and the best response to this was a quiet assurance of the kind Stephen Decatur could show perfectly, so convinced was he that he would soon either be dead or a hero — one or the other, no in between.

From the deck, Commodore Preble had seen the *Enterprise* coming in, and he was as eager to hear the news that Decatur brought and to learn what had happened, as the lieutenant was to tell him. But the commodore had his own special dignity, and it ill befitted him to behave like a schoolboy, gawking along the rail as one of his ships came in. So Preble coughed and hied himself to his cabin, where he buried his head in the latest group of dispatches from the Secretary of the Navy — all of them urging rapid action to put an end to the Barbary pirates. The most recent of the dispatches indicated some official displeasure in Congress over the capture of the *Philadelphia* and the failure of the squadron to recapture it or to regain the national honor in some other manner.

"Damned busybodies," snorted the commodore. He would not, of course, have said that to one of his officers, but in the privacy of his cabin he had little use for politicians. He was musing on how half of Congress would look hanging at a yardarm, when he heard the piping, and was suddenly conscious of the coming of his favorite young lieutenant with a prize and news. He buttoned his uniform jacket, and put his nose back into the correspondence. When the marine guard at the door announced that Lieutenant Decatur was there to see him, the commodore kept him waiting five minutes, just so the young whippersnapper would not get too big for his britches.

Then, with a grunt that was supposed to indicate total disinterest, he told the guard to let the lieutenant in, he was ready to see him.

"Well," he growled. "I see you're back. Learn anything?"

"We captured a prize."

"Oh?"

"She was one of the gunboats that did Bainbridge in."

"Well, that's something. Maybe we'll be able to have her sold. That would be prize money."

"With all due respect, sir, I think we ought to keep her."

The commodore shifted and looked up, half angrily.

"You do, do you? And for what reason, if I might ask?"

"I want to take her in and bring out the *Philadelphia*."

"The hell you say."

Lieutenant Decatur was used to the rude responses and apparent angers of his superior, and he sat, stolidly, never cracking a smile or frown, and waited. The commodore fidgeted, looked him up and down, and grunted.

"Well, tell me what's on your mind. It can't hurt to listen."

Decatur then told the commodore of what he had seen through his glass that cold foggy morning off Tripoli, and how he felt it quite possible to take the *Mastico* in with a volunteer crew, move through the surrounding gunboats that looked just like her, swarm aboard the *Philadelphia*, cut the cables, and run for it, fighting their way out of the harbor if need be. For an hour he laid out his plan, showing maps and details that he had drawn and put together in the past two days at sea.

Preble scratched that long jaw as he listened, and he did not interrupt, which Decatur knew was a very good sign that he had the commodore's full attention and interest. At the end, the commodore snorted.

"Damned impudence," he said. "You young fellers think we can risk half the fleet on some harebrained maneuver you dream up while you're floating around at sea. No. I don't believe you can bring the *Philadelphia* out in the daytime, and I know you can't do it at night. End up on the rocks again, and then we've got another crew in the Bashaw's jail. More hollow laughter from Washington — and my neck in the noose. No, thank you, sir."

"All right," said Decatur, swiftly. "I'll accept that situation. Then let me go in and burn her. That I know I can do."

"You know. You know. The trouble with you

puppies is that you think you know things that real seamen forgot about before you were dry behind the ears. But I'll say this much — there might be a chance of it. How are you going to get in there?"

"Sail in. At night."

"And who's your pilot?"

"Myself."

"Oh." There was immense ridicule in the commodore's voice. "You know the tides? You know the currents? It has been your habit to sail in and out of Tripoli harbor in the past two months?"

Decatur flushed. "No, sir. But I have been by that harbor mouth three times, once with you, sir, and I have good enough eyes. I know I can make it."

Preble softened. "Look, boy," he said. "You know you can make it, and I, the Lord help me, may even believe you could do it — you've got backbone enough — but I cannot risk the lives of a hundred men — ."

"Seventy, sir. That's all it would take."

Preble glared at the interruption.

"— I cannot risk the lives of seventy men, if you would have it, on a scheme that the Navy Department and Congress would call ridiculous on the face of it." He glared, and Decatur sighed inwardly, his heart turned to lead. He rose to leave.

"But I'll tell you what I will do," said the commodore, rising with him. "You find yourself a pilot who knows Tripoli harbor, and you get him in here, and we'll talk about this again."

"Yes, *sir!*" cried an ebullient Stephen Decatur, as he flashed the commodore a salute, and very nearly tripped over the musket of the marine guard as he hustled out the door and headed for the boat rail. Down the boat stairs he sped to his gig, and grinning like an idiot, he leaped aboard.

"Well, boys," he said, "tonight I want you in every tavern on the waterfront, and I want you to turn me up a pilot who knows Tripoli harbor like the back of his hand."

"That we'll do gladly, sir," said Abby Tyler, who was also captain of the lieutenant's gig. He rubbed his hands together. "And maybe there's a bit of prize money coming up soon?"

"Not a chance of it. The *Mastico* is going to become a warship. We're going to use her to give the Bashaw a taste of Hell."

"That's just fine, sir," said Bosun's Mate Tyler, holding his face together. "Just fine. We'll be down on the wharf tonight, and we'll find you a pilot, sir."

"Maybe this will help you," said Decatur, flipping him a sovereign.

"Why thankee,sir. It will. It will." Tyler pocketed the coin and the others nodded solemnly. That sovereign would keep them in wine and grappa all night long, the crew of them.

Stephen Decatur did not let on in any way that it was the last sovereign he had to his name, and very nearly the last bit of cash. For he was a generous officer, and pulled more than his share of the ship's wine mess, helping the younger officers and particularly the midshipmen, whose niggardly pay allowed them virtually nothing to drink at all, except ration rum. And he bought so that the mess of the *Enterprise* was far better, wardroom and fo'c'sle, than any other ship her size in the Mediterranean. So, as he had tossed that gold coin so lightly to Abby Tyler, Decatur was like the gambler at the royal tables in Syracuse or Messina, who staked his last bit of fortune on the card of chance.

Back aboard the *Enterprise*, he began questioning his officers, to see if they knew a merchant captain or anyone in Syracuse who could lead them to a Tripoli pilot. But they did not. And there were things to be done. The *Mastico* had to be taken in to the quay, and her prisoners handed over to the royal authorities of the Two Sicilies. Here in Syracuse, by treaty the Americans had full rights, but they would retain them only as long as they did not abuse the hospitality of the Sicilians, and Preble was punctilious in his diplomacy. So the report was made, and the prisoners decanted, and the *Mastico* brought back out to anchor behind the *Enterprise*. This work and the hospitality that must be accorded the Sicilian chandlers who came aboard to see what the young capitano would require, now that he was home again — for Syracuse was his second home, was it not? — and the sampling of the wines the chandlers had brought to sell took up the rest of the afternoon. Decatur hadn't the heart to tell them that even if he emptied his pockets, he could not have bought a bottle of the red, let alone a cask of Marsala. But let them wait a bit — if this venture was successful there would be wine enough for everyone and glory enough for all.

That night, a rowdy boat's crew made the rounds of the harbor tavernas, dropping bits of Lieutenant Decatur's sovereign here and there, drinking his health noisily and toasting their ship and the "damnedest captain that ever sailed the seven seas."

It was nearly eleven o'clock, six bells on the dog watch, when they broke into song and very definitely showed themselves as Americans. Sitting at a table in the Mercedia, a combination grog shop and restaurant that was frequented by many merchant sailors, they were a noisy crowd, but not belligerent, and they aroused a benevolent smile from most of the mates and supercargoes of merchant ships in the place. The Americanos were welcome enough — their money was good and their manners less grating than those of the Englishmen who thought they owned the sea.

Abby Tyler was leading them in singing a shanty, a rather indecent one, when suddenly, out of nowhere, there appeared at their table a short, slender man dressed in the loose shirt and trousers of an island sailor. He stood quietly, unsmiling, until Tyler interrupted the song.

"What can I do for you, mate?" asked Abby Tyler.

"You are the Americans from the ship of Lieutenant Decatur who captured the *Mastico*?"

"That's right, mate. We're the ones."

"Can't you see the word hero written all over us?" piped up Shorty Calmer, able-bodied seaman, twenty-two years old, and carrying a full head of steam stoked by Sicily's hot wine.

The slender man bowed. "I am sure you are heroes. Mustapha Rais was a very strong and very courageous captain."

"You knew him?" Suddenly Abby Tyler was quite sober.

"Very well. In fact I was in Tripoli harbor on the day that he brought in Captain Bainbridge of the *Philadelphia*. It was a sad day for freedom of the sea."

"Say, who are you?" asked Seaman Calmer.

"Salvatore Catalano of Palermo."

"You a merchant or something?"

"I am fortunate enough to be captain of a small vessel. It belongs to an English firm, if you will pardon me for saying so. We trade from here to Malta, where I once lived."

"You a Sicilian?"

"No. I am Maltese, a British subject, they say."

"And you've been to Tripoli?"

"I go there once a month. The Bashaw has a fondness for Sicilian wine."

"Then you know the harbor?"

"Intimately."

"You're our man." And so saying, Abby Tyler stood up to his six feet four inches, swept the Maltese under one arm, half lifting him off the floor, and headed for the door. "Pay up, Cronky, you've got the money, and let's get back to the ship. The lieutenant will want to see this man."

3

In port it was Lieutenant Stephen Decatur's habit to spend the first night on return from a voyage aboard the vessel, ignoring the captain's prerogatives of command in favor of sending his junior officers ashore to let off steam. This habit gave him a chance to know his crew intimately in their most unguarded moments, and to know his ship as few captains knew theirs, the cranks and the little differences that meant no two vessels were ever just alike. So he was aboard, chatting with Lieutenant Joseph Bainbridge, the brother of that poor, unlucky man locked up in the Bashaw's castle, when Abby Tyler and the boat crew swept raggedly up to the ship, with such a racket that Decatur knew there was more than simple drunkenness involved.

"We've got 'im, sir," said Abby Tyler, climbing the Jacob's ladder on the starboard side.

"Got whom?" asked Decatur, smiling, as he leaned over the rail and peered down into the boat.

"Your pilot, sir."

Decatur's heart leaped. He had not really expected so much, at least not so soon. "Well, bring him aboard, boys." He peered down again worriedly. "You haven't hurt him?" He knew his raucous sailors, and if the pilot had given them trouble . . .

"Not a hair on his lovely head, sir," said Abby Tyler, grinning. "We didn't even have to tie him up. When I said you wanted to see him, he came along quick as a leave boat headed for the Battery. It seems he wants to see you, too, sir."

So a wrinkled and bedraggled Salvatore Catalano was hoisted up the ladder and virtually thrust into Lieutenant Decatur's arms. A smile, an apology, an indication of the importance of Catalano in Decatur's life, and the past half hour was forgotten, as Decatur grasped the Maltese by the arm and led him to his cabin, where he produced a decanter and glasses.

"So you know Tripoli harbor?"

"Since I was eight years old. I've swum around every one of those reefs — there are eight of them — and my grandfather was once the Bashaw's father's armorer . . ."

"That's enough," grinned Decatur. "I see you know the place. Now, what is more important — how do you *really* feel about the Bashaw and the taking of the *Philadelphia*? I know you're an English subject, but what you say will go no further than this room."

Catalano looked across the table at this vigorous young man who so casually asked him if he cared to put his neck in a noose. Why should he trust him? If he were to say that he had been

31

much impressed with the capture of the *Philadelphia* he would be telling no more than the truth — and he might also end up in irons in an American brig. But somehow, the intent look and the open countenance before him indicated that he could trust this man.

"I was impressed," he said cautiously.

"Of course, you were," said Decatur. "I would not have believed you if you had said otherwise . . . But do you have any real loyalty to the Bashaw?"

Catalano began to make a rude gesture, then remembering that he was in the American's cabin, he suppressed it, but not before Decatur saw and noted.

"He cut off my grandfather's hand," he said. "He did not like a suit of mail that fit too tight — he had gained twenty pounds since the fitting — so he cut off my grandfather's hand."

That was answer enough, and Decatur pressed no further.

"I want to go into Tripoli harbor and burn the *Philadelphia*."

Catalano gasped. "They have at least fifteen gunboats surrounding her."

"Sixteen. I counted them two days ago."

"And each of those gunboats is manned by the Bashaw's hand-picked fighters."

"They are indeed vigorous men. We have come up against them."

Catalano recalled the image of Mustapha Rais, a hulking blackbeard, quick with scimitar and dagger. Then he thought about how this young man who smiled so sweetly had wiped Mustapha Rais from the face of the earth.

"I am a cautious man," he said tentatively.

"An excellent attribute," agreed Decatur. "Have another glass."

Warmed by the Marsala, and by the agreeable disposition of the young lieutenant, Salvatore Catalano began to see merit and possibility in the idea of burning the *Philadelphia.*

"It will take many brave men," he said.

"I have a hundred. All will volunteer."

"And a stout ship."

"We will use the *Mastico.*"

"And many rapid combustibles."

"We have whale oil and rags, and plenty of dried wood, and vitriol."

"And we must have help."

"We shall have a ship to escort us."

"Then there is a chance."

"That is all we could ask for, agreed? And you."

"I . . ." Catalano hesitated.

"All I ask you to do is to draw us a chart of the harbor, with every obstruction, and with accurate readings on the tides and currents."

"I would like to come," said Catalano firmly. "I owe the Bashaw this favor."

Decatur seized his hand across the table. "Agreed," he said. "There will be much glory in it, and perhaps some money if we are lucky."

"I am not interested in the money," said

Salvatore Catalano, pausing and swallowing hard, for what his mouth had just uttered, his ears could scarcely believe. "I do this for revenge."

"And you shall have it," said Decatur. "Now let us draw a plan."

Giving Catalano paper and ink, he watched as the Maltese merchant captain sketched a plan of Tripoli and her harbor. There, on the point, were the French fort and the line of batteries that guarded the walled city from the open sea to the west and north. Batteries and mole ran around the spit and headed southeast, and behind them was the town, with the castle of the Bashaw at the most protected point. Down to the east behind the shoals, lay the English fort, and protecting it all were the reefs that extended out from the mole line to the northeast. Forts, reefs, batteries, and gunboats made Tripoli a very strong bastion.

Then Catalano showed the route they might take, coming in from the northeast of the reefs, and skirting around through one of the channels that led between the shoal water and the reefs outside, pointing directly down the throat of the castle. Just a few yards off the castle the *Philadelphia* was anchored, between her and the outer harbor was a nest of gunboats, and at least the English fort would be able to bear its guns on any vessel that approached her. The French fort and the batteries could not fire until the raiders started out again — assuming they were able to effect a surprise entrance of the harbor.

Late that night, very late, the captain's gig went ashore once again, carrying with it Signor Catalano, with the promise that he would keep his mouth sealed — and to make sure of it and of the man's safety, Decatur sent with him a marine guard to watch his door.

Next morning, the ship, alive and cleaned for the day, and captain's mast over with — for it was always a short procedure with Decatur — he took the gig to the *Constitution* again. He was piped aboard and presented at the commodore's cabin.

"So soon?" asked Preble. "You've found your man?"

"My boys found him," said Decatur. And then he sat for an hour sketching out what he wanted to do and what he would need to do it.

Preble listened carefully. He did not tell Decatur that weeks earlier he had suggested to the Secretary of the Navy that the *Philadelphia* be destroyed; that he had simply been waiting for the right man and the right time to do it. He grunted and nodded so many times that Decatur was not sure he was making himself understood.

But at the end, the commodore leaned back, put his hands behind his head, and gave one of his rare smiles.

"Well done, boy," he said. "You have a simple workable plan. And if you can get the men to volunteer, I think you have a chance of carrying it off."

"No trouble, sir," said Decatur.

"Oh?"

"I mustered the men this morning and asked for volunteers."

"And?"

"Every man jack."

"That's a far cry from Gibraltar," said Preble, remembering only too well why he had moved the squadron, for every night there had been deserters and malcontents going over to seek the protection of the British flag, and getting it without question. "You must have a stout ship."

"We think so, sir," said Decatur, with just a touch of pride.

The commodore coughed, and growled. "All right, now get down to business. I shall draw the orders, and you shall have Stewart in the *Siren* to help you. He'll be disappointed. He wanted to do it himself, but you got there first — and with a pretty good idea."

Decatur went out, walking on air. What he did not know — what the commodore had not said, and what he did not say to anyone, was that when he had written the Secretary of the Navy he had told him that he feared the cost in lives would be great, but that the end of the *Philadelphia* was worth the loss. Decatur was expendable.

4

Lieutenant Decatur, with the urge of youth, had expected the orders to come immediately. They did not. He sat and fretted and wondered. And finally he made inquiries through the commodore's aides on the *Constitution* and discovered that the Old Man had no intention of sending him out until spring. That meant March, and this was the end of January. The news came as a shock, but with the acceptance of discipline he had learned on the *United States* and practiced on the *Essex* and the *New York*, he settled down to wait.

The social season of Syracuse was at its height. The city, old and weathered, was the provincial capital as well as the principal seaport of the region, and its nobility went back to Roman days. The Marchese di Montalto was the social leader of the town, and his palazzo was the scene of many a ball in that winter of 1804. Of course, the Americans were invited — the young naval officers made a grand show wherever they went in their blue and white and gold. Syracuse was also port of call for the British when they came this way, and they managed to come often enough, to keep an eye on these waters and their archenemy, Napoleon Bonaparte. The salons were filled with discussion of the collapse of the Treaty of Amiens, because the British would not surrender Malta to the Knights of Malta. Fighting was breaking out on land and at sea, and the British officers who came to call in Syracuse were most resentful of the Americans, France's old allies of the revolutionary days.

Moreover, there was still this sophisticated air of superiority. The officers of a British man-of-war, pulling into Syracuse, expected the chandlers to rush to them, to find them the berths for their ships, to push and pull and haul about any and all who might be in the way of His Majesty's representatives.

But the Sicilians were used to the Americans, and found them far easier to deal with than the haughty British. Their failure to jump and carry infuriated the men of the Royal Navy, so they went about Syracuse looking for trouble, and this meant the lower decks, and the quarterdeck. Three times in one month Lieutenant Decatur had to go ashore to rescue his sailors from the local authorities. Fighting with the British — it was always the same story. And if Stephen had to appear stern and unforgiving on the wharf, when he got back to the ship it was double rations of rum for those involved.

It was almost as bad in the salons, where the officers congregated. The Marchesa di Montalto held court on Wednesday evenings, and it was the habit of the Old Man to go there, and he encouraged his young officers to go also. It would do them good to have a taste of European manners and society, he said, and their brave appearance could not but help the flag.

On the Wednesday following his discussion with the commodore, Decatur finished up the day's work, not hard in port, and wondered whether or not to go ashore for the party. He decided against it; his dress uniform threatened to become threadbare, and so far from home, even if his father was a fairly well to do merchant captain, Decatur did not feel like worrying the family about money. No, he would pass this one up.

As dusk fell, he was musing over his plans for the *Philadelphia*, when the *Enterprise* was hailed by the *Siren*'s boat. A sailor came to tell Decatur that Lieutenant Stewart was alongside and wanted to talk to him.

Now, properly speaking, this was the worst of sea manners, even if Stewart was his superior. But Charles Stewart and Stephen went back a very long way together. In Philadelphia days, they swam the Delaware, attended Dr. Abercrombie's academy, having the hard lessons of Latin and mathematics knocked into their tough heads, and hunted in the woods outside the city. So when Charles Stewart came alongside and hailed in his languid way, too damned lazy, as he put it himself, to come aboard and pay the usual amenities, Stephen was not the slightest bit upset. He went to the rail, hung over like any paltry merchant captain, and began a conversation with his friend in the boat below.

"Are you going to the marchesa's?"

"I didn't think I would tonight."

"Come on along. The *Warsprite*'s in today, and there'll be a gang of Horatio's boys on hand. I need protection. Maybe even from impressment."

"You need protection like I need a wife."

"That's true, too, Stevie. Come on along. Seriously, we might learn something about what old Boney's up to."

"All right," said Decatur. "Give me a minute."

"You're a captain. Bring your own gig. Well, ta ta, as we say in Westminster. I'll see you on the quay."

Stephen stepped down into his little cabin, and found that Andrews, his cabin boy, was there before him, that his black boots were polished, and the blue dress coat laid out on the narrow bunk. The trousers he was wearing would do, a clean stock and he was ready to go after a wash. He clapped the heavy hat on his head and shouted to Abby Tyler to bring the gig, but as with so much in Decatur's life, the men were way ahead of him. "He treats us well, by God," said Abby to the boat crew, "and we can do the same for him as long as he's with us. 'Cause he's not going to be on this little tub for long, mark me Monday."

So the boat was waiting when Decatur came on deck, and he went down the ladder like a schoolboy, and leaped into the sternsheets and sat in one motion. In five minutes he was at the quay. He grinned at his crew, told them to hang on till he came back. "Now mind you, one man will stay with the gig, and you'll all be relatively sober when I return."

"Aye, aye, sir," said Abby Tyler.

As Decatur turned away he could hear them talking. "Which one is going to stay . . ." that was the voice of young Brattin, the apprentice seaman.

"Quiet, young 'un," said Tyler in a fierce whisper. "He didn't assign anybody anythin'. We'll take turns."

And so they would, Decatur knew, putting away incredible quantities of that snarling white grappa that burned throats raw. And when he came back they, would at least appear to be sober.

Arm in arm, Decatur and Charles Stewart walked apace through the narrow, crooked streets of the old town, keeping to the middle, but with an eye overhead, for the slops came down from time to time and it was best not to be in the way.

Soon enough they arrived at the palace, set right on the street in the manner of the old houses, and they were given entry by a pair of guards who knew them as part of the American force that was anchored in the bay. They went up the stairs, through a brightly lighted foyer, and a reception room, where they were greeted by the marchesa's major domo, and led into the big ballroom, where the tables were stacked with food, and liveried waiters moved around with glasses of wine and punch.

The place was well crowded already, with the blue of the Americans mingling with the blue of the British, and the red and green of the Two Sicilies regimental officers, and various diplomats and nobles and their ladies. The women were dressed magnificently, in their silks and satins, long ball gowns that swept the floor, and great hoops and gathers of material.

Some wore powdered wigs in the old style, but most had hair that was either their own, or made to appear so, piled bouffant atop their heads. Pearls and diamonds, rubies and emeralds glistened on their arms or against their cleavages, for the style of the day was a low-cut bodice gown that was most revealing. And these ladies were veritable models of the fashions of London and Madrid.

The Americans headed for the little knot of men around the Old Man, over in the corner, drinking punch and holding forth on the issues of the day. The British were off in another corner, talking among themselves. The Sicilians, too, tended to gather in little groups of their own.

Decatur stood off a little to one side, listening to the commodore and his discussion of Napoleon. He was at that moment talking with the British consul. Suddenly the marchesa herself came bearing down on him, a young woman in tow.

"My dear Lieutenant Decatur. Let me present him, my dear — he is one of the most eligible bachelors of all the Americans, and as handsome as you are beautiful. The Contessa d'Amalfi."

Decatur raised the young woman's hand to his lips and as he did so caught a glance at her face. She was most striking. Coal black hair framed a pale white face, with straight nose, generous lips, and flashing dark eyes. She was tall for a woman but three inches shorter than Decatur, and the décolleté gown revealed an ample figure, the tight stays pinched in a delicate waist.

She was blushing.

"You are incurable, auntie," she said in French. "You must stop flinging me at the head of every young man in Syracuse."

"My poor niece is a widow," said the marchesa. "Happily married for only a year, and then the count was killed in a hunting accident. Now she has just come out of mourning."

"I am sorry for your loss," said Decatur, his eyes fixed on the girl's face.

She shrugged. "It was the will of God. My little daughter and I have adjusted."

"But she must marry again. She must," said the marchesa. "And I am recommending to her an American because I believe she would love your country."

"Please, auntie." The girl's black eyes flashed,

and she colored again. "What will the lieutenant think?"

"Only that you are the most beautiful and charming woman in the room," said Decatur gallantly. "Come, may I get you some punch?"

She took his arm, and he led her to the table where the servants were dispensing sweets and punch. They proceeded then to chairs on the side of the room, and sat, discussing the Barbary wars and Stephen's career to date, although of course he said nothing of the *Mastico* or the plan for the *Philadelphia*.

They talked then of her life, and her interests — horses and literature and music. And they spent a pleasant half hour together.

"I must be going soon," she said. "For it is nearly my daughter's bedtime and every night I tuck her in."

"May I see you home?'

"I would be most pleased."

Just then, a tall man dressed in the uniform of a lieutenant in the British Navy moved forward. He was blond and wore a monacle screwed in his right eye. His face was slightly red, as though he might have had too much punch, although he carried himself well, and spoke firmly enough.

"Teressa," he said. "I've been looking all over for you."

The girl was cool. "Derek," she said in acknowledgment. "May I present Lieutenant Decatur of the United States Navy, Lieutenant Rosmore of the British Royal Navy."

44

Decatur bowed, the English officer nodded briefly.

"Decatur. I don't believe I know the name. It's not English."

"No, French. My grandfather was an officer in the French Navy. He decided to settle in America."

"One of those blasted Huguenots, I suppose," said Rosmore.

"Lieutenant Rosmore is third son of Lord Rosmore, one of England's leading Catholic nobles," said the contessa.

"That's right, a good Roman, just like Teressa. Come, may I take you home?"

"I am sorry. Lieutenant Decatur is seeing me home."

"Oh? Well, these Americans do move in, don't they? Be careful of him, Teressa, they say the Americans have a girl in every port. Racy types."

"Sir," said Decatur, with a note of warning in his voice.

"Ah," said Rosmore distantly. "I've insulted you. Touched a raw nerve, I suppose. Bad joke."

"Your apology is accepted — this time," said Decatur.

"Apology? I . . ." but the British officer caught the look in Decatur's eye, and wandered away, mumbling to himself.

"There, now I've caused you to make an enemy," said the contessa, ruefully. "You must be careful of him. He is a famous duelist, with sword and pistol."

"I thank you for your concern," said Decatur, "but do not worry about me. I shall do my best to avoid trouble with him or any other man."

She put her hand on his. "Do be careful. I think I would not like to see you hurt."

They found their outer garments, the lady's cloak and Decatur's greatcoat and tall hat, and moved out into the street.

"I do not keep a carriage," said the contessa. "I live only three streets from here, and the old city is so crowded. So we walk."

Walk they did, the three blocks to the large stone building that was the contessa's palazzo; not so ornate, and not nearly so large as the Palazzo di Montalto, but an impressive building.

"My husband's," said the contessa. "It has been in the family for three hundred years. Would you care to come in?"

They entered. A manservant in livery took her cloak and the lieutenant's greatcoat and hat, and they moved into a pleasant drawing room. She rang, and a servant came.

"What would you like? Wine? English tea? I suppose you have dined? You navy men eat so very early."

"I have not."

"Then do stay and eat here with me. It gets very lonely, and I would be grateful for your company. But, you must occupy yourself for a little while. Go, try the library." She pointed to a door across the room. "I must go and say my goodnights to poor little Caterina. It is hard being mother and father, you know."

Decatur wandered into the library as the contessa left the room and mounted the stairs. He twirled the huge vellum-covered globe and glanced idly at the books on the shelves, rich morocco and light polished leather bindings, books in English, French, Italian, Spanish, and languages he did not know.

He took down a volume and leafed through it, and then suddenly, he smelt the fragrance of jasmine, the same fragrance he had sensed when he had kissed the contessa's hand, and she was in the room.

"They are good books," she said. "I read them a good deal, for they help to pass the time. But I am intruding my unhappiness on you too much. Come, let us go in to dine, and you shall tell me about your family and your home in Philadelphia. Odd, it is a famous Greek place, as this once was, or named for one."

They dined, sitting at the huge baronial table, he at the end, where he was certain her husband had once sat, and she on his right. The servants came silently, brought a magnificent meal, poured wine, and departed as silently. They talked and talked, until finally, Decatur started.

"You must pardon me. I am so rude as to examine my watch." He pulled forth the gold hunter from his waistband. "I have a boat crew waiting at the quay, and I cannot leave them there."

"Of course, duty," she said, nodding.

"Yes. Duty before pleasure, before self."

"And with you I can see it will always be that way. The woman you marry will have much to accept."

"You may be right," said Decatur.

"But she will be a very fortunate woman, nonetheless," said the contessa, coloring, speaking intently.

He was silent.

"I will see you to the door."

They walked slowly, for he was loath to leave the company of this charming and beautiful woman. And at the door, she secured his coat and hat for him and waited while he donned them.

"You must come again," she said. "I have told Caterina about you, and she wants to meet you."

"How old did you say she was?"

"Two." She laughed. "Well, if she were older I am sure she would have said so."

"I shall come."

A cloud crossed her face. "And be sure you are very careful of Lieutenant Rosmore."

"Yes."

Then, as he was turning to leave the house, she came to him, and suddenly was in his arms. He embraced her, but drew himself away, taut with longing.

"I absolutely must go," he said.

"I know," she said. "But I want to be sure you will come back. To me."

He touched his lips to her face again, then waved and smiled as he went through the door into the street, and without looking back, strode toward the quay.

5

Decatur's path to the ship took him by the Palazzo di Montalto once again, and as he drew opposite the entrance he could see that the soiree was still in progress. He hesitated, but remembered his purpose and did not pause in his stride as he moved past the doorway, where carriages were still drawn up. But a few feet beyond, he was hailed from behind.

"Lieutenant."

He turned. It was Midshipman Macdonough of the *Enterprise*.

"Good evening, Mr. Macdonough. Going back to the ship?"

"Yes, sir. I saw you and thought perhaps . . ."

"That you could beg a ride in the gig? Of course. I'm pleased that we've met. I can recall many a night shivering on a wharf waiting for someone who had a boat to come along and take me back to the *United States*."

Macdonough's face brightened in this reassurance that a man who had reached the lofty rank of lieutenant could recall those distant days when he was a mere midshipman and had no privileges.

"Thank you, sir. I am very grateful."

They walked along in companionable silence, through the twisting streets, their leather heels clumping on the cobblestones. The city was quiet. A few lights shone in houses, upstairs, but it was nearly midnight and doors were securely locked, bars thrown, and windows bolted up against the danger of the Sicilian night. Syracuse was a port, and like others it had more than its share of robbers and brigands who preyed equally on men at sea and on the land when they might.

The two young officers, in dress, their great-coats dark against the night, might have been a pair of roistering noblemen. Their swords were concealed beneath the long coats.

Perhaps it was for this reason that suddenly they heard scuffling of feet around a corner. Decatur's experience in many ports brought him up short. He put a restraining hand on the midshipman's arm.

"Your sword," he whispered fiercely. Aloud he spoke with the accent of a man far gone in wine.

"Whash the trouble there, mister — amigo —" he said. "Come on, 'shnot far now. Lesh go."

Meanwhile he was unbuttoning, and had his sword in hand, and Macdonough had done the same. Then they moved to the center of the street, and turned the corner.

Before them five men stood, in a pattern that completely blocked the street, and each had a

51

weapon in his hand. The central figure, muffled in black, carried a long sword.

"Stop," he said in Italian. "We will trouble you for your wallets."

"Whashat?" Decatur mumbled as he moved forward, sword concealed behind him, and Macdonough copied his superior.

The dark man took a step forward, as if to grasp Decatur by the arm. "Drunken sots," he muttered. "We'll have no trouble with them."

"Oh," said Decatur clearly. "I would not say that."

He whipped his sword forward, and before the dark man could move, he had impaled his right arm. The wounded man's sword clattered to the cobblestone, steel ringing.

"I'm stabbed," cried the leader of the gang. "On them, men. Don't let them escape now." He fumbled in his garments for another weapon, but Decatur now turned the flat of his sword, and smashed the man across the nose. He crumbled to the ground, senseless.

The other four were moving in, clubs, dirks, and short swords in hand. Macdonough engaged one, and wounded him slightly, but another came from behind.

"Quick!" shouted Decatur. "The wall. Get over there and get your back against it. We must have fighting room."

They ran to the wall of a small park, faced on the other side by a darkened three-story house. Placing their backs squarely against the stones, they cut and parried, and kept the four brigands at bay for ten minutes. Their leader, who had recovered, now stood back and urged his men on, as well as he could through a mouth of broken teeth.

"Get them!" he shouted. "They must not escape. Honor demands revenge."

Decatur slashed, parried, slashed, and ran one man through the chest. With a gentle sigh, the man dropped his bludgeon, and sank to the ground. With Decatur's move to attack his second assailant, that robber dropped his knife and ran along the cobbled streets. The leader, seeing how matters stood, fled. Decatur turned now to Macdonough's aid. The two remaining brigands took to their heels.

"Are you all right?" Decatur asked the midshipman.

"I think so. A little scratch on the face."

"That'll be something to talk about in the mess. Come on along. Let's get back to the ship before we get in any further trouble."

They moved down the street then, and past the entrance to the house. There was scuffling, and the door opened. The dark figure of the leader ran up the stairway of the house. Macdonough was after him in a moment.

"No!" shouted Decatur. "Don't be a fool. You don't know what's in there."

But the midshipman was not listening, lost as he was in the pursuit of his enemy. Decatur followed slowly, watchfully. On the second landing he heard the pounding of footsteps above, and as he rose to the third, the tinkle of breaking glass. On the third floor he found himself staring onto a balcony, Macdonough on the outside, leaning over and looking down.

The midshipman was obviously shaken. "I . . . I . . . He ran out on the balcony and I came out and he just jumped." He shuddered.

Decatur was soothing. "What's the difference? If he had fought you, you would have run him through, and if he had not fought, he would soon be in the hands of the green coats, and they would make short work of him."

"I suppose so," said Macdonough doubtfully. "But it seemed so sudden."

Decatur was sympathetic to the man, but outwardly he showed no concern. Macdonough must be toughened for the events to come.

"Never concern yourself with how your enemies are destroyed," he said. "As long as you behave honorably, and effectively. This fellow was headed for a bad end. You just helped him along."

As they descended, the pounding of feet was heard on the pavement below, and by the time they were on the street, they were surrounded by green-clad carabinieri of the governor's police force.

"What is going on here?" demanded a fierce young lieutenant of police, whose long mustaches did not conceal the fact that he was even younger than Decatur.

"We were set upon by thieves," said Stephen.

The lieutenant looked down at the two bodies in the street, and kicked one, then the other. The man Decatur had wounded groaned.

"You have done us a favor, signor, in eliminating these monsters of the night. Were there others?"

"Two."

"I must apologize for the governor of Syracuse, but on the other hand I must also ask you to come with me to the station of the police. It is against the law to kill people on the streets."

"It was self-defense."

The lieutenant spread his hands.

"I have no doubt of it. Nevertheless the law is the law and particularly since you are foreigners, it must be followed. There is much criticism at Naples because of the Americanos."

So Decatur and Macdonough were carefully, even courteously, escorted to the police station, and held there in a long room, equipped with several hard chairs and a table.

"Excuse me," said the police lieutenant. "Our facilities are not really adequate for distinguished guests." He brought a candelabra and set it on the table. "Would you care for wine, or something to eat?"

The two Americans refused, and the lieutenant bowed and excused himself again. They sat and they waited for a full hour before they were released. Then in the anteroom of the police headquarters they found an angry Lieutenant

Dent, the commodore's aide, arguing with the police lieutenant. As they emerged, the conversation ended, and Dent escorted them outside.

"I guess your gig is still on the quay," he said. "I told your boys what happened, but they refused to go back to the ship."

They walked on in silence for a moment.

"For some reason," Dent continued, "these people seem to want to make an issue of your killing those ruffians."

"What does the commodore say?"

"He would like to tell them to take the deep six," Dent grimaced, "but he is also supposed to be a diplomat, so he is waiting it out. He thinks the British are putting the governor up to it. They want every harbor in the Mediterranean for their quarrel with old Boney."

"And I guess they don't much want us around here either," grinned Decatur. "Well, maybe we've heard the last of it."

"Let's hope so," said Dent. "The commodore said to tell you not to worry."

"I hadn't even thought about it," said Decatur.

By this time they were at the quay, and an eager Abby Tyler was rousing the crew of the *Enterprise* gig. So they parted, and went back to their ships, in the deep dark quiet of the Sicilian night.

6

Next morning, Decatur received a note from the commodore, as he was instructing his midshipmen in the use of the sextant. He turned the task over to the first lieutenant and walked back to the poop to read the message and see if it required an answer. It did not.

"Under the circumstances," the message read, "I think you had best take the *Enterprise* out for another look at Tripoli harbor. I am meeting the governor this afternoon, and it would be just as well if I could report you absent on official business."

The issue was more serious than he had expected. Who would believe that a fight in self-defense against a gang of thieves would bring such trouble? Decatur was worried, not for himself, but for the difficulties in which the United States might find herself because of the politicking. There was nothing that he could do, except obey orders. He put down the note, and began to prepare the *Enterprise* for sea. The Old Man would not want a written answer. What he would want was to see the *Enterprise* moving out of the harbor within the hour, and if she did not, the commodore would suggest that perhaps another lieutenant would keep his ship ready for sea.

He would do one thing: he would send Lieutenant Lawrence, his second in command, to the flagship to report to the commodore saying he had been detailed by Decatur to begin arming the *Mastico* for the coming adventure. On the face of it, the Old Man would be madder than a wet sea hen over such impudence, but Decatur was banking on the commodore's realization, once he thought of it, that if Decatur came back with the information he expected to have, the expedition against Tripoli would have to be staged a good deal earlier than March.

So Lawrence was detached and told what he must do, and he went ashore, grimacing at the thought of what the Old Man would say.

The usual procedure in moving out of harbor was to sail with jib out past the mole and then to hoist mainsail and get under way. But with a swift sailor and sure ship like the *Enterprise* this wasted a good deal of time, and to show the commodore how much in a hurry and how sprightly he and his men could be, within half an hour, the *Enterprise* was ready for sea. For the work of moving in and out of shallow water, she had been rigged as a staysail schooner, two jibs, two staysails from the foremast, and the big triangular main. A good northeast breeze was blowing through the harbor as Decatur ordered anchors raised. The stern anchor was raised first, letting the ship hang from the bow, into the wind, with the flying jib and jib set. That was usual procedure. But as the bow anchor came up, the next orders were not usual procedure.

"Ready to hoist upper stays'l, hoist away. Ready to hoist stays'l, hoist, ready the main, bring her up boys" — and the *Enterprise*, pretty as you please, answered her helm, shivered a little as the wind caught the canvas, heeled, and headed on a broad starboard tack directly past the flagship. In a moment they were by, so close they could see the gaping of the men at old *Connie*'s rail as the little schooner sped past, under full sail in the middle of Syracuse harbor.

"There'll be hell to pay for that," said James Lawrence to himself as he sat in the sternsheets of the boat that was taking him to the *Constitution* to report. But he was wrong. When the commodore emerged from his cabin, the *Enterprise* was just inside the mole and changing tack. The Old Man simply looked out and snorted.

"Boys will be boys," he said. And that was that.

Nor was he upset, after one quick shocked look, to learn that Decatur had dispatched his second in command on a task that by law could only have been assigned by the commodore himself. "Good idea," the commodore grunted, and issued the orders that would enable Lawrence to begin provisioning the *Mastico* — vitriol, oil, gunpowder, and pitch, that would certainly burn anything made of wood.

"Get hold of that feller Catalano," he grunted at Lawrence. "He'll know how to load her up. And when Decatur gets back here, tell him I want to see him, and he'd better also have a new name for that ketch. I'll leave it up to him. He'd name her anyhow, if I didn't." The Old Man smiled — his schoolboys were his trial and his hope, for with them he was helping refashion a badly abused American Navy.

So Lieutenant Lawrence set about provisioning the captured ketch, while Decatur headed southeast toward Tripoli.

As night fell, along with the clouds of dusk came a change in the glass. Before moonrise the sea was covered with a thick layer of winter fog. They were outside the normal lanes of sea travel, cutting across to make Tripoli, and not worried as much as a larger ship would be about shoal water if they came close inshore. But the fog was a different matter, and Decatur, for all his derring-do and youthful enthusiasm, was a careful captain who did not risk a ship. The *Enterprise* lay hove to for a watch and a half, the lookouts listening and craning at every fancied sound, Decatur, having posted his watches himself, since he had left Lawrence behind, retired to his cabin, with full confidence in his crew, and threw himself on the bunk, to drift off to sleep immediately.

At four bells on the morning watch, he was

awakened. He opened his eyes immediately, as he always did, but he did not know the source of the noise that had roused him. Then he heard his lookout in the forepeak.

"Sail ho. Bearing on the starboard bow."

Pulling on boots and his uniform coat, he set the hat atop his tousled hair, and headed for the deck. Forward, through the lowering mist he could see the outlines of a ship, a frigate by the look of her, not an American, but a 36-gunner that might be British, or she might be French for all he knew. Then came a hail.

"What ship?"

"United States schooner of war *Enterprise*," shouted Decatur in return. "What ship there?"

"His Majesty's frigate *Warsprite*," came the reply. "I am sending a boat."

"What for?" asked Decatur, across the narrowing gap between the ships.

"Information you're carrying deserters," said the other voice, an odd voice, one Decatur almost thought he recognized. "Who's your captain?" the voice spoke again.

"Lieutenant Stephen Decatur, United States Navy," said Decatur. "Who's yours?"

"None of your business, Yank," said the other. "You stay hove to. We're boarding."

Decatur did not answer. Instead he issued a series of low-pitched orders, and soon men were scurrying along the decks of the *Enterprise*, carrying lighted matches, held low so they would not be visible across the water, and carrying muskets, pikes, and cutlasses.

The British frigate stood close in, lazily, her gunports closed, and scarcely a man on deck. This pipsqueak of an American schooner was not worth even calling the men to general quarters. It was nothing more than a routine investigation, and Captain Babcock, Royal Navy, was yawning in his greatcoat as he stood on deck and waited for his boat to return. He would not have stopped this little vessel had he not need for five seamen. Those wretches of No. 4 gun had decided to desert in Syracuse harbor, and while he and his officers had been engaged at the Palazzo di Montalto they had slipped overboard, swum ashore, and disappeared sure as snuff. There were always Eyeties out in the back country who would take them in. Half anarchist, that's what they all were anyhow. He sniffed, and wished he had a good cup of tea with a tot in it to ward off the sciatica. This infernal fog!

As the British boat drew near, Decatur stepped to the rail. There in the stern he made out the form of an officer and then recognized him. Lieutenant Rosmore.

"Hello, Yank," said Rosmore, mockingly. "Trot 'em out."

"Trot who out?"

"Our deserters. You've got five men from a British man-o'-war aboard you there, and we've come to get them."

Decatur was cool as ice. "Put one foot on United States property and I'll blow your boat out of the water, lieutenant. You keep your impressment parties off my ship."

And as Decatur spoke, all twelve guns of the little schooner were manned and the burning matches held high to show the British boat and the frigate beyond.

"We'll blow *you* out of the water," shouted an infuriated Rosmore.

"Not before I hole the hull of that frigate a few times and sink your boat," said Decatur. "Ready to fire, men, ready on command. Sails up, let's go."

It was the same maneuver Decatur had used when he left Syracuse harbor — even the slight breeze that was carrying away the fog was enough to bring the little schooner into motion, and before the shocked eyes of the captain of an impressive 36-gun frigate, and the empty hands of his boarding party, the *Enterprise* sailed off on a broad reach, into the wispy blackness.

Abby Tyler, who had spent many an hour coaching the men to respond to these unusual orders of their captain, heaved a happy sigh as they ran into the fog and escaped the sight of the frigate, which was just then beginning to open its gunports.

"Now, that's what I like to see," he said to no one in particular. "Twist the lion's tail."

7

As the sun came up, the sky cleared and the warming air whisked away the mist before the *Enterprise*. She sailed south and tacked east toward Tripoli. The day was fine and visibility extended to the horizon, but there was nothing to see; not a ship crossed their path or even came within masthead view. The sun brightened, the brisk southeast wind drove them along so that the taffrail log line was taut and the cutwater left a very satisfying stream on each side of the bow. She was sailing as well as she ever had, and she was a beauty; indeed the Secretary of the Navy had commissioned a shipbuilder to put up two more schooners just like her.

At six bells on the day watch, they passed the point where Tripoli should lie, just over the horizon, and Decatur headed further east, for he wished to come up close inshore and the wind had shifted around to the east. If he kept his course he would be tacking as he neared the enemy city, and he would be in an unfavorable position to do battle. This way, driving downwind, he had the advantage and could fight or not, as he pleased.

Prettily, the *Enterprise* turned, as land showed on the horizon. They were not far from the spot where Bainbridge had gone aground in the *Philadelphia*. These waters were dangerous and full of reefs, but little *Enterprise* drew only a little over five feet, less than half by far of the draft of the bigger ships, even when they were lightly burdened.

Sailing up along the coast, close in, was dangerous business. The Tripolitanian gunboats were fast, and they could shoot through the holes in the reefs with amazing speed to attack. But Decatur wanted a close look at the *Philadelphia*, and he was determined to have it. They sailed up next to land until the tall crenellations of the English fort appeared, and then moved out to a safer distance. There was no sense in being a fool, for the guns of the fort could be expected to train on them as they passed, and if they were too close in and were recognized as Americans, the guns would most certainly begin to fire. Months earlier, Commodore Preble had regularized the "war" with the Bashaw by declaring a blockade of Tripoli. In fact it was no blockade at all, for the American squadron was not strong enough — particularly with the loss of the *Philadelphia* — to maintain constant surveillance of the ports. But the state of siege regularized the capture of the *Mastico* and vessels like her, and also gave the Bashaw an excuse for firing on every American ship.

As they cut inside the Kaliusa reef, where the *Philadelphia* had struck, Decatur turned seaward. The maneuver would bring him just opposite the *Philadelphia*, where she lay in the deep harbor almost due east of the Bashaw's castle. There she was, he saw her, riding nicely at anchor, heavy enough in the water that he was sure she was provisioned, and the last of the canvas seemed to have been rigged and all the running rigging was in place. He wondered if the Bashaw's men had been able to gun her properly. He did know from secret dispatches that Bainbridge had managed to smuggle out of his prison that the crew had managed to throw the ship's guns overboard before the capture.

As he came within good view of the ship and assured himself that she could sail at any time, he heard the shriek of shot in the air, the report of a gun, and saw a splash off to port. Then came another. Smoke showed at the side of the *Philadelphia*. They were firing at him, by God — and from an American ship. The Berbers had recovered the guns of the *Philadelphia* from the water, no doubt about it.

If the gunners were good, and that first near miss indicated they were, then prudence dictated a retreat. Decatur turned to starboard, heading out to sea. He had learned even more than he had expected. Preble would have to advance the mission. No one could guarantee the time when the Bashaw would send the *Philadelphia* out to begin her depredations of the commerce flowing into Malta and Syracuse and Sardinia.

Sailing north, toward Malta, Decatur kept his eye out for enemy craft.

Late in the afternoon, just as the purpling sky made lookout difficult, his men spotted a sail. It was downwind of them, and they began to overhaul. The other ship, a raked-mast craft that indicated Berber design, ran before them and tried hard to escape, but she had no advantage in canvas or hull, and although her captain was a good seaman, it was scarcely an hour before Decatur was in hailing distance, and prepared to board.

"What ship and where are you bound?"

"We are only little traders, signor, and we are going to Malta."

"What are you carrying?"

"A few hides, some wine, a little fruit."

"Stand by for a boat."

The captain, in his filthy turban and dirty shirt, simply shrugged and gave an order. The big sail dropped, and the craft lay hove to in the water, the last rays of sun glinting across her decks.

Decatur led the party himself. He wanted to see just how this vessel was laid out when at sea, for she was uncommonly like the *Mastico* and when he put out from Syracuse in a few days he wanted to excite no suspicion. He clambered aboard, in lead of the party, and began to look around.

He must be able to do better at least in cleanliness, than this captain. For if he had appeared disheveled from afar, close up he was filthy indeed. Decatur would have wagered that a thousand fleas crawled under that shirt.

A dozen men were similarly attired, in loose shirt and voluminous trousers, drawn at the waist by sashes instead of belts, and various headgear, from caps to turbans. They squatted on the deck, Eastern style. Decatur wondered if any of his men could sit on their heels thus, perfectly balanced. He was not sure he could do it himself and vowed to practice in the privacy of his cabin. But the answer was to look lazy, that much was sure. There could be none of the spit and polish of the western sailor. Languid was the word.

Purely in routine, Decatur had sent Macdonough below to look over the cargo. Suddenly there came a shout from the lower deck.

"Lieutenant. I've found something."

Decatur narrowed his gaze on the captain, who licked his lips, then suddenly, like a cornered wolf shouted. The squatting men came surging forth, daggers and bludgeons in hand, to attack the American boat crew.

"Take them, men," shouted Decatur, drawing his sword and lunging at the captain, who now produced a scimitar and sprang at him. Decatur parried the blow with his scabbard — sword not yet completely free, then dodged around the wheel. The captain pursued, but by the time he had managed another slash, Decatur's sword was out, and steel rang on steel. Then a parry, a cut, a lunge, and Decatur drew blood. With a cry, the captain of the pirate ship fell back, and then clenching his teeth and muttering, he charged again, mad with bullish rage. Decatur slashed downward with his sword, and the edge bit into the man's neck. Blood flowed down the dirty gray shirt, the captain fell to the deck, and his eyes rolled once around in his head. Then he died.

Stephen looked around him. Three other members of the crew were lying in pools of blood on the deck, and the men of his boat crew were standing over them. Another half dozen Arabs cowered in the poop, prepared to have their throats slashed and be thrown overboard — for that would have been their way had they been the victors.

Decatur headed for the cabin, and there he found Midshipman Macdonough standing over the body of another Berber, examining a sheaf of papers, a sword and scabbard in his hand. Macdonough handed him the sword.

"Bainbridge's," he said, significantly. "Along with these." He held up a sheaf of papers, including several drawings of the *Philadelphia*. The papers were in Arabic.

"What is it?"

"As far as I can figure, it's some kind of statement about the *Philadelphia*. And before this fellow died," he nudged the body, "he said they were on their way to Algiers. What do you think, sir?"

"I think the Bashaw is trying to link arms with the Dey. Let's get under way and back to Syracuse. This is a matter for the commodore."

So the prisoners were put under close guard aboard the *Enterprise,* and the prize crew, under Macdonough, sailed the *Serena,* for that was the ketch's name, back to Syracuse, following as close as possible in the wake of the American schooner. And sailing in, Decatur hardly waited for the stern anchor to be dropped before he was in his gig, heading for the *Constitution.*

"Well?" said the commodore, when Decatur had seated himself.

"I saw the *Philadelphia.* They've got the guns back aboard her, and they've got gunners who can shoot." He described the firing on them by the double-shotted gun.

The commodore stroked his chin, and said nothing.

"I think we had better go in right away," said Decatur.

"You do, do you? Well, you have been thinking that ever since you proposed the idea."

"But then I didn't have these," said Decatur, drawing forth the papers taken from the *Serena.* "If you can get them translated, I'd wager they will show that the Bashaw is trying to make a deal with Algiers. And with the two frigates, they would have something."

The commodore took the papers. He examined the maps, and he rang the bell on his desk. The marine guard came in, and saluted.

"Take these to Mr. Dent and tell him to get them translated." He turned to Decatur. "You might just be right, and if so, we will send you in to take the *Philadelphia*. Be ready."

The interview was over. Decatur stood, gave a salute, which the Old Man returned absently, and went smartly out the door. As he passed through, Preble called after him. "By the way, you might make a call on the *Mastico*. Have you got a name for her?"

"Yes, sir. I want to call her the *Intrepid*. That is what she is going to be when we take her into Tripoli harbor."

"All right, boy. That name will be in the orders. Now you go on over there. Your friend Catalano has been busy, along with Stewart and Lawrence while you've been gone. She ought to be just about ready for sea."

Decatur gaped. So, the Old Man was one jump ahead of him again. Well, that's what it took to be a commodore, and it was worth understanding. His heart light and his tread high, Lieutenant Stephen Decatur went back to his ship, dreaming all the while of high adventure.

8

For three days, Decatur labored mightily to make the *Intrepid* thoroughly ready for sea. The whole crew of the *Enterprise* volunteered for the job of burning the *Philadelphia.*

"You know," said Decatur, as he addressed the men, "that some of us — a lot of us — might not come back. If necessary we'll fire the *Intrepid.* We either make it by the boats, or we swim for it, or we don't make it at all."

"We'll make it, lieutenant," shouted Abby Tyler from the rear row. "With you in command, there's nothing to fear."

A thousand pounds of gunpowder were bagged in fifty-pound bags, and Decatur laid out a plan of the *Philadelphia.* Then he made assignments of squads of men to place the powder in the vital spots. Others were to take the pitch, and others the tightly corked bottles of vitriol, which would be thrown into the flames, along with the oil, and oil-soaked rags would be laid against the sails. The men were counted off into squads; ten officers and sixty men. There was no shortage of willingness or of direction. Lawrence would go, and Lieutenant Joseph Bainbridge, the brother of the captain shut up in the Bashaw's castle. Lieutenant Jonathan Thorn would command a unit, and so would Macdonough, and five other midshipmen, and Surgeon Lewis Heerman would go along to doctor the wounds of any who were hurt.

Commodore Preble issued the orders, but he did not deliver them yet. He found that Decatur's guess had been correct — the Bashaw was trying to negotiate with Algiers for a naval union against the Westerners. He found that he agreed with Decatur's insistence. But still he waited, for until the *Intrepid* was ready for sea, there was no need for haste.

Pilot Catalano, for he had signed himself on now to make this voyage as the pilot, spent many an hour below the decks of the new American warship, supervising the pitch-painting and calking of the boards. Her planks were sound, but she had been badly handled and needed attention. Accustomed to this type of vessel, and knowing how to get the utmost from the local workmen of Syracuse harbor, Catalano was as good as a naval dockyard superintendent in getting the work done and done right.

At the end of the third day, Catalano reported to Decatur, his face long.

"We've got rot in the bottom," he said.

"How bad?"

"Not so bad as long as the ship doesn't have any strain. But if you were to bump the frigate or another, there are two bad planks down by the keel that might tear out."

"How long would it take to fix her?"

"Two days. Maybe three."

"Make it two."

So Catalano hurried off, and the *Intrepid* was hauled that very afternoon, and two of her planks torn out to be replaced.

Decatur reported dolefully to Commodore Preble that it would be two more days before he was ready to sail.

"All right," said the Old Man. "Here are your orders. They're sealed until you get out of harbor. Stewart will take the *Siren* with you, and you're to have Midshipman Anderson and nine men from her. As for the rest, you can read what I want done when you sail, and I'll leave it up to you. Good luck, young man."

Decatur left, clutching the orders in his hand, and went back to the *Enterprise.* The waiting was too dreadful to contemplate, and as he paced his deck, he recalled the promise to return to visit the contessa. Almost without thinking, he went below to his tiny cabin, washed in the metal basin, shaved, donned a clean shirt, stock, and the pressed jacket laid out for him, and headed ashore.

"Return the boat," he told Abby Tyler when the crew landed him at the quay. "I'll be late and I'll find a bumboat to bring me out."

He strode quickly the short distance to the Amalfi residenza, and knocked the huge brass knocker against its pedestal. The manservant who came was polite and unruffled. If the lieutenant would wait a few moments, he would see if the countess was receiving.

He paced nervously back and forth in the drawing room where he had sat with the contessa that evening that seemed so long ago. Then she was in the room, a new scent this time, one he did not know, but it met his nostrils with a charm and grace that quite fitted her beauty. She was dressed in pale blue, gown, slippers, and hair veil that stuck up above a high comb in the Spanish style that was popular that season. The cut of the dress again emphasized her firm bosom and tiny waist, and the flash of little slippers beneath the gown added to the pretty picture.

"Lieutenant Decatur. How charming to see you again." She was very formal.

"I could not stay away," he said.

"It is a great compliment to pay a lady," she replied.

My God, thought Decatur. Is she going to start this now? Fencing?

"You were a long time in your return," she said tentatively. "The press of official business?"

"I went to Tripoli," said Decatur, hating himself for revealing so much, but feeling the need to reestablish reality between them.

Her hand went to her throat. "To fight?" she said.

"A little. A very little. By the way, I encountered your friend on the high seas. Rosmore.

He tried to board me."

She gasped. "And?"

He shrugged. "Nothing. We did not wish to be boarded by a Britisher, so we sailed away."

"Just like that?" She snapped her fingers.

"More or less."

"Lieutenant, you amaze me. You take your little ship — what do you call it — schooner — and you beard a British frigate and you sail away from them just like that," she snapped her fingers again. "You are either a great fool or a great hero."

"Fool, I suppose," said Decatur, reddening. "But we Americans do not like to have our seamen impressed into the British Navy."

"No." She was touched. "And you will endanger your lives to prevent it."

"That is our job."

"You take your career very seriously, my friend. I wish I knew more people who believed in things strongly enough to fight and even die for them."

"Rosmore?"

"He is nothing but an English snob."

"I had the feeling that he was more to you."

"He would like to be." Her eyes flashed. "A young widow with inherited estates has many admirers."

"Especially if she is beautiful and kind."

It was her turn to flush. "Why thank you, sir. I believe you mean it."

An embarrassed silence fell over them. The intimacy had come quickly, and suddenly there was nothing to say.

"Would you like to see my daughter?"

"Very much. Does she resemble you?"

"Not in the slightest. She is the image of the Amalfis."

They walked up the stairs, along a corridor, and into a large chamber, where a little girl sat on the floor, playing with dolls, a maid watching over her. The contessa picked her up and cuddled her, and showed her off. "This is my baby, lieutenant. She is a good baby, is she not, Coletta?"

The maidservant smiled. It was obvious she adored both baby and mistress. The little girl looked shyly at Decatur, put her finger in her mouth and hid her head in her mother's bosom.

The contessa laughed and gave the child back to the maid. "She is a little witch. She will be a temptress some day."

"Like her mother."

"Come, sir, your compliments are too much for me. They turn my head."

It was the mocking again — but this time Decatur knew he had earned it, with his clumsy line of talk.

"I'm sorry," he said. "I did not mean that. It was rude."

"No," she said. "I know that young girls love this fencing, and I did myself. But when one has experienced great tragedy, and life is real — such talk becomes meaningless."

"I promise never again to say anything I do not mean."

"Then we can be friends," she said, taking his hand. "And I need friends. I have too many admirers. Too many Rosmores who want either estates or" — and she blushed — "something else they are sure a widow would want to give."

They returned to the drawing room.

"I would ask you to dine," said Decatur. "But there is no place. My ship cannot accommodate a lady, even for dinner — the wardroom is absurdly small" — he made a gesture, indicating a box. "I have no clubs. I am a foreigner, and quite at sea."

She laughed. "It is no problem. I would have you dine here this evening, but I must go to my mother-in-law in the country. And I shall be there tomorrow. Could you come? The estate is lovely. We might even have a picnic if the weather is fine."

Decatur calculated. Catalano said two days. That meant the morrow and the day after. And although he could be busying himself on the *Enterprise*, he knew from watching Lawrence and Catalano and the others that he would be a fifth wheel. His job had been to set in motion, and it would be to act. But in the interim, let his capable assistants alone.

"I would be delighted."

"And you could stay the whole day."

"At least until nightfall. I should return to my ship then."

78

So it was settled. Next morning, at eight o'clock, he would be on the quay, and she would send her mother-in-law's carriage to bring him to the estate, some twelve miles from the city. The conveyance would be at his disposal in the evening, to bring him back to the ship.

"You are really most kind to an itinerant."

"I told you," she said. "I need a friend."

9

Next morning, Decatur arose humming, for reasons he did not quite understand, and he was unusually jovial for Decatur in the morning. It was Saturday, the day of captain's mast aboard the *Enterprise*, but he looked over the list of offenders.

"They're all volunteers," he said to First Lieutenant Lawrence. "Let's let them off this time, and tell them why."

The pumps were just being secured and the decks were still wet when he called for the gig. He was ashore waiting on quay at eight o'clock sharp, when the gray and maroon carriage of the Amalfis pulled up behind two spirited horses. They stood, the condensation steaming from their nostrils in the morning chill.

It was a fine day for the end of January. The sun was out and promising, with scarcely a cloud in the sky. Decatur wore his greatcoat, but was sure that by noon he would discard it. He was also sure from the promising weather that an outing, or at least a walk in the countryside, would be part of the entertainment. He could use it, he mused, as the carriage jogged roughly over the cobblestones of the city. It had been many months since he had been out for a long hike. The life of a sailor was confining; he walked enough, but it was back and forth on his little deck. Even on the gundeck, the length of the vessel was only eighty-four feet, which meant from the poop sixty-two turns plus the length of the ship to No. 1 gun to make a mile.

He noted absently as they left the city that the cobblestones ended with the gate through the city wall. They were on a well-traveled road now, and the horses let out a little, moving smoothly with the grace of their breeding. Life was so simple for these European aristocrats; they had their pick of horses and ladies, and their wealth seemed endless. Even a second or third son, like Rosmore, bore the unmistakable stamp of his breed — spoiled, confident, even arrogant; made so by half a dozen generations of wealth. Well, he would a dozen times rather be an American, where he, grandson of a French immigrant, could aspire to any position he wanted. Lawrence, whose father was a Tory, and his friend Stewart, who began life as a tanner's apprentice, could aspire as high as he. It was a grand flag to serve under, to fight under, even to die under.

Such thoughts coursed through Decatur's head as he considered the coming expedition against Tripoli. He went over the plans for the attack again and again, until he felt there was little chance of error.

At the end of half an hour the horses slowed. The coachman turned them off to the right into a long drive flanked by an eight-foot stone wall. The Amalfi estates, most certainly. Driving in, half a mile, Decatur mused that it must have taken a hundred men almost a year to build that wall. No such thing existed near Philadelphia, nor in all the United States, that he could imagine. There was a difference. Americans had better things to concern themselves with than the trappings of great wealth.

The drive broadened out, through a grove of big bare trees, and the rambling white building with its red tile roof came into view. The coach moved slowly up to a portico, and stopped. The footman jumped down and opened the door, and another appeared to direct Decatur inside the hall.

"I shall announce you, signor," he said, smiling. "The contessa has been waiting."

She appeared, dressed this day in a rough wool costume that set off her pale white face and shining long black hair. She took both his hands and pressed them warmly.

"I am so glad you could come today," she said. "I did not tell you, but it is my birthday."

Decatur's face showed his distress. "And I have brought you nothing."

"You have brought me yourself," she said. "See, I can be as gallant as any gentleman. No, seriously, there is no present I could wish today. I am a happy woman."

Decatur thought it odd that she, so recently bereaved, could be so carefree. But as they walked about the big house, and she showed him the works of art, and the family gallery, and the park behind, he sensed that she truly was happy. He watched as she spent an hour with the baby. Her face broke often into laughter, and she cuddled the child to her with little expressions of love that could not have been feigned. Then, when it was time for little Caterina's nap, she handed her back to the nurse, and led Decatur purposefully to the pantry behind the grand dining room.

"They have a hamper for us. We can go into the park, and beyond, where my father-in-law keeps his little hunting lodge. It is chilly for eating outdoors. But there is a kitchen there, and the walk will be pleasant today. Or perhaps you would prefer to ride? I could change."

"No, thank you," said Decatur. "My sea legs have enough trouble without asking them to hold a horse. Let's walk."

So arm in arm, he carrying the basket, they walked through the woods along a bark trail. At the end of a mile she sat down on a log, gasping.

"I must do this more often. I don't get enough exercise these days, living in the city. But look at you, you are not even breathing hard. And you confined to a ship most of the time."

He told her then, about the sixty-two turns he made twice a day plus the other seventy-two feet to make a mile, and she laughed at his precision. She laughed, too, at his tales of Abby Tyler and

Cronky, the cook, and the other men of the ship who lived the devil-may-care life of the professional sailor. By the time they reached the lodge, she was pink and bright-eyed, and he knew very well that it was not assumed.

They ate, then, sitting on the steps in the sunshine, the cheese called provolone, and the biting Segesta wine of the area, a cold meat pie, and a sweet. And when they had finished, she leaned back against the shingle siding and sighed.

"It is a long time since I have enjoyed a day so much," she said gravely.

Decatur hesitated. She looked at him.

"You think it odd that I should be so happy, when I am a widow?"

He nodded.

"He was a brute. I hated him from the first moment. The marriage was arranged by my family. The old story, estate and position, promises that it would not matter what he did. But it did matter very much. He had women, a hundred of them. But then he was killed — a drunken accident — and I had Caterina. It was a tremendous relief to me."

"But don't you grow lonely?"

"A little. Loneliness is a blessing compared to that life." She shuddered, and impulsively, he drew her to him. They embraced, and she was in his arms, fierce, passionate.

Later, they returned down the long path in the gathering gloom of late afternoon, and in the mansion, Decatur was presented to a pleasant woman in her sixties, Teressa's mother-in-law, who looked upon him with a benign eye and inquired if they had enjoyed their outing.

Dinner would not be until eight-thirty, because the old count was detained in the city on affairs, and Decatur said that it would be too late for him to stay. Regretfully, he took leave of Teressa, at the door.

"You have given me the happiest day of my life," said Teressa, clasping his hand. "Please let there be no regrets, nor any feelings of obligation. I am content. And if we see one another again, let life find its own course for us."

The dowager contessa in the background, there was no time for more tender parting. Decatur responded with a firm pressure of his own, a smile, and the promise that though he would be off on a new mission in a few hours, he would call on her upon his return.

She waved the carriage out the drive, then turned, and went back into the house walking steadily and with the light step of the carefree.

Decatur's thoughts were awhirl after this strange, wonderful day. But the jogging of the carriage brought him back to reality, and soon his mind was turning again to the adventure that lay before him. He went over the whole plan — an officer for every six men lessened the chance of error to the point where they *must* succeed. There would be no desertions, nothing of the kind that had plagued the squadron since its arrival in the Mediterranean. Just this day he had heard that more than a hundred of the men of the *Philadelphia*, shut up in the castle, were appealing to the British to get them out — saying they were in truth British subjects. Such callousness, such lack of love of country was hard for Decatur to understand. True, the discipline on some ships was far too much like that of the Royal Navy to please him, but that was no excuse for a man denying his birthright in hope of escaping imprisonment.

Such thoughts occupied Decatur on the half hour's journey back to the city through the dusk. It was growing dark when the carriage pulled up beside the quay. Decatur's eye moved to the harbor, where he expected to see the familiar outline of the *Enterprise*. But a ship had interposed itself, a frigate if his training was correct. Suddenly he knew it must be the *Warsprite*.

Down from the carriage, Decatur was saying his thanks to the coachman, when a voice came from the shadows.

"Well, popinjay, I see you are keeping fine company these days. The Conte d'Amalfi's carriage, no less."

He turned. From the shadows appeared the lean form of Lieutenant Rosmore, voice mocking as he came forward.

"And what have you been doing today, sailor boy? Dabbling in the sweet waters of love with the beautiful Teressa?"

"Mind your tongue, lieutenant," said Decatur. "My affairs ashore are no concern of yours. And I shall trouble you not to use the Countess of Amalfi's name as you are doing."

"Ah, touchy, aren't we? Again the rude Rosmore tongue strikes home. But your affairs at sea are my concern, ducky. Especially when you turn and run away from one of His Majesty's ships on business of the crown. We'll get you yet, and we'll have those deserters from you."

Decatur shrugged. "You'll get a shot in the belly if you try to board my ship again, lieutenant. Nothing personal. You or any officer of your government. We'll not have impressment of Americans aboard my vessel."

"Brave, aren't we, when we are ashore and just back from an afternoon of diddling. I'd like to see you say that again at sea . . ."

Decatur did not wait for the British officer to finish. He moved forward, his right arm cocked, and he drove a smashing blow into the mocking lips that split the flesh and felled the officer like a log. He stood back then, waiting for Rosmore to rise. "Next time you make any reference to the Countess of Amalfi in my presence I shall kill you," he said quietly. "Remember that."

"You'll have your chance, you blighter," muttered the British officer, a kerchief to his bleeding lips.

"I shall relish it," said Decatur. Stepping around the Englishman, he headed for the water, calling for a bumboat to take him out to his ship.

10

Next morning, the challenge came, as Decatur had been expecting. A boat came alongside the *Enterprise*, and hailed. A lieutenant Decatur did not know came forward as Decatur moved up from the cabin.

"Lieutenant Rosmore presents his compliments, and asks what weapons you would prefer."

"I shall refer you to my second, sir. Lieutenant Lawrence will act for me."

"That is good, sir," said the other. "I am Lieutenant Downs of His Majesty's service. I shall be acting for Lieutenant Rosmore."

Decatur turned, to let Lawrence make the arrangements, but something, a not unfriendly look in the British officer's eye, suggested that the other had more to say. He turned back.

"Let me warn you, Mr. Decatur. Rosmore is a dead shot."

The suggestion was clear, the British lieutenant was very intense.

"Thank you, sir," said Decatur gravely. "I shall confer with Lieutenant Lawrence, if you will give us a moment."

When Lawrence came to him, he said in a low voice, "Pistols at four paces."

"Four paces, Decatur? My God, he can shoot your eye out."

"And I his," said Decatur calmly. "They will be his pistols, and I'll not have a chance to gauge them."

When apprised of Decatur's choice of weapons and distance, the British lieutenant started, then looked back at Decatur's grim face, and bowed to him as he left the ship. "You are a man of courage, sir. I wish you luck."

So, Rosmore was not so very popular among his own officer contingent, if a lieutenant he had never before seen would both warn him and wish him good fortune in so desperate an encounter.

The duel would be staged at dawn in a field ten minutes from the center of Syracuse. That was decided and the word passed from Lawrence to Lieutenant Downs. Surgeon Heerman would attend Decatur, and the British officer would bring his own doctor.

The news coursed through the American squadron that day, and when it came to the attention of Commodore Preble, he was not pleased.

"Damn it," he said. "Get Decatur over here. I'm running a naval operation, not a dueling society. Doesn't he know better than to jeopardize the job he's got to do tomorrow?"

Decatur went to the flagship before noon, not without fears of his own. The Old Man's temper was well known. What if he decided to give the Tripoli job to Stewart?

The commodore erupted as Decatur came into the cabin.

"Goddamn it!" he shouted. "How many times have I told you to stay away from trouble with these limeys. We've got a job to do here. You are not, repeat, not a schoolboy any more."

But when Decatur had explained the source of the argument, or at least part of it, for he left Teressa's name completely out of the matter, the commodore's rage subsided. Or, rather, it changed its point of focus.

"Well, that puts a different face on it. They're growing high and mighty with their pickoffs. Maybe there are some Britishers in the naval service, but if so there must be good reason for their desertions. Not that I countenance desertion, of course, but I'll not have the limeys poking around my ships."

Gruffly, he dismissed Decatur, with a plaintive note that perhaps he could refrain from knocking British officers down in the future, if he got out of this one with his whole skin.

"If you get yourself hurt now, you know Stewart will get the job," he said.

"I know that, sir," said Decatur with a confidence he was far from feeling. "I'll not get hurt."

Back at the ship, tension growing, Decatur whiled away the afternoon. Then, late in the day, a bumboat approached the *Enterprise*.

"Hey, fend off there, amigo," said Abby Tyler

in what he hoped was Sicilian. "What do you want with us? This is an American ship."

"Questa è *Enterprise*?" asked the voice. "Capitano Decaturo?"

"Yes, yes," said the bosun's mate, and the boatman handed up a letter, addressed to Decatur, which Tyler hastened to deliver.

Decatur took the letter. It was heavy with scent, with the coat of arms of a family embossed on the envelope.

He opened it and scanned.

"My dear," the letter read. "I write this in haste and fear, for I have heard from our coachman of the incident at the quay, and I know that he will challenge you. He is a deadly shot, and almost as good a swordsman, and he loves to kill. So my heart quakes as I address this. But may I ask, for my sake, that even though all I say is true, you will somehow protect yourself and refrain from hurting him."

There was no signature. None was needed.

Decatur had been pondering his course. His first impulse had been to shoot for the eye. Rosmore was an arrogant fool and deserved to die. But his own conscience had pricked him; Teressa did not know, although she might have guessed, that Decatur also was an expert with pistol or with sword. Long hours of practice on the Delaware, firing at debris in the water, had sharpened his eye, and longer hours of sweating lunge and retreat in the sail loft of the Smith company's warehouse had strengthened his arm and made his sword sure.

Teressa was asking what only a woman would ask — that he protect himself and not hurt the other fellow. It was nearly impossible, but it put the clincher on Decatur's own decision.

He dined late, so much the better to pass the time, undressed in the little cabin, and got into his nightshirt as if he was relaxing. He was awakened at an hour before dawn, and dressed swiftly, shivering in a cold that was not allayed by the bucket of coals brought from the galley to warm his cabin.

As they were rowed ashore, Lawrence sat glumly in the thwarts, Heerman on the one side and Macdonough on the other. Decatur sat in the sternsheets and looked around him, without any visible sign of emotion.

"I shall shoot the gun out of his hand," he said as they clambered out of the boat. "And if there is a second shot, I shall shoot him in the arm."

They moved into a public carriage that Lawrence had hired for the occasion, and in a few minutes were at the edge of the big field, poplars surrounding them. The light was just beginning to break through the skeletons of the trees. There was no wind. That much was good, Decatur thought, although at four paces wind was not a great problem.

They took position in the middle of the field and waited. In half an hour, the Englishmen came, stopping their carriage a hundred feet from the American conveyance. Then, seeing the figures in the field, they hastened to join them.

Decatur bowed coldly to Rosmore, who smirked at him, and bounced a ball up and down in his hand. The Englishman seemed about to make some taunting remark, when a scowling Lieutenant Downs nudged him and pulled him away.

The duelists drew pistols from a leather box held by Lieutenant Downs. Lawrence examined the gun, and the charge, removed the ball, looked it over, and reloaded. He looked at Decatur and nodded. All was well.

The opponents were led to the center of the field, and placed back to back. Their seconds then moved away and flipped a coin to see who should give the signal. Lawrence won.

"I shall give the order, one, two, three, four," said Lawrence. "On each count you shall take a step away from the other. On the count of four you are free to turn and fire at will."

Decatur stood stock-still, pistol at his side. He noted the sudden rise of the wind. He must make a small allowance even at four paces.

Lawrence cleared his throat.

"Ready, gentlemen."

Decatur nodded. He could not see, but apparently Rosmore did the same.

"One."

Decatur took a pace, carefully, swiftly. He must remain steady and smooth, and ready to raise his arm as Lawrence said that last word, then turn and fire, almost without aim.

"Two."

Another step. The vision of Teressa's face swam into Decatur's mind, her worried look, the beauty of her eyes.

"Three."

Teressa was wiped away by a scowling commodore, shaking his finger and saying, "For God's sake, don't get yourself hurt."

"Four."

Decatur stepped forward on his left foot, swung around on his right and planted it firmly in front of him. He raised the pistol as he moved, and sighted on Rosmore's weapon. He fired. As he pulled the trigger he felt the rush of Rosmore's ball across his neck, and the burn of it. A little more to the right and he would have been a dead man.

But then Rosmore's gun disintegrated, and he stood, a cry escaping his lips, blood pouring down from a shattered hand.

"You bloody bastard," he shouted at Decatur, before the surgeon came up, and Lieutenant Downs turned him around and led him away.

Lawrence moved to congratulate Decatur, but he waved him off.

"See if he wants another shot," said Decatur. His second moved across the field, where the English contingent was huddled about Rosmore, the surgeon dabbling and opening his kit. Surgeon Heerman took a professional look at

Decatur's neck, and snorted.

"Well, nothing wrong with you. You could have cut yourself shaving worse than that."

Across the field, Lawrence was grim as he approached Lieutenant Downs.

"You know your man delivered another insult," he said.

Downs looked very unhappy and said nothing.

"My principal wishes to know if you want another shot," said Lawrence, unbending.

"Rosmore's hand is shattered. He will never shoot again."

"We could demand further satisfaction under the circumstances," said Lawrence.

"I know. I hope you will not."

"No. Lieutenant Decatur would never take advantage of any man, not even a boor," said Lawrence, and although Downs flinched at the word, he was careful not to bridle, for it was a deadly moment.

Lawrence hesitated one moment longer, looked at the pitiful Rosmore, who was holding his hand and swearing, gesturing wildly as the English surgeon tried to quiet him. Then the second walked back across the field and turned to Decatur.

"Well, you fixed him. He'll never kill another man with a pistol. At least not with a pistol in his right hand."

"Perhaps he has learned something," said Decatur, "although I doubt it. At least he will be more careful now." The face of Teressa came into his mind again, and he was content. He had served her, and he had served himself well.

Just how well came to light that day as the news of the duel moved from scuttlebutt to scuttlebutt among the ships in the harbor.

"By God," said Cronky Willet to Abby Tyler, "He says he's gonna shoot the gun out of Mister Britisher's hand, and then he does it, cool as you know."

"It was an accident," piped up Seaman Masters, who had shipped aboard not two weeks ago.

"Accident, my nose," said Abby Tyler, clenching his fist. "This'll teach you what's an accident. Decatur's the best shot in the American navy, barring maybe Captain Barron of the *New York*. Don't you go saying accident to me again."

So the word was out that Decatur had coolly chosen his point of aim and had shot the man's fingers off, just as he had said he would, and soon the story was moving throughout Syracuse — and Decatur's marksmanship was given so much attention that some were even expressing sympathy for poor Rosmore, the victim of the famous American duelist.

"That's life for you," said Lawrence, as he and Decatur shared a bottle of wine, in the captain's cabin. "They warn you that he's a killer, and then when you disarm him, they all go weepy about it."

"Rosmore is no fool," said Decatur, "loud-mouthed and arrogant though he may be. I doubt if we have seen the last of him."

11

Next morning Decatur was called to the flagship to pick up new orders. Typically, the commodore had been thinking about the project and had some changes. It was just eight hours before he was to sail.

"It's you," said the commodore, as Decatur entered the cabin. "I see you're all in one piece. I'm surprised. That feller was supposed to be the King's Prize with a pistol."

Decatur said nothing.

"I think you must have spooked him with that four paces. Not gentlemanly, you know. Not the thing to do. Americans are supposed to conform to the limey's rules and stand and get shot at. Smart bit of work."

And that was all that was said about the duel. No threats, no recriminations. The Old Man, in his way, was a very understanding commander. He knew the problems the ship captains had to put up with, facing their British cousins.

"Well, are you all ready?"

"I think so, sir."

"Damn well better find out, don't you think?"

"Yes, sir. We are ready. Salvatore Catalano

has his charts. He knows the channel into harbor like the back of his hand. Here's my plan for the burning of the *Philadelphia*." He leaned across the desk, placing a drawing in front of the commodore, and began tracing with his finger.

"We'll go aboard amidships, probably on the starboard side, for she is likely to be heading into the tide, and Catalano says the current swirls around just here. Lawrence and Midshipman Macdonough will each take six men aft, port and starboard. Lawrence will set fire on the gundeck, to burn through the rudder cables. Macdonough will fire her in the aft ammunition and powder stowage. Then . . ."

"That's enough. That's enough," said Preble. "I can see that you know what you're talking about. All right, so by some miracle Catalano gets you in there, and you fire her. How are you going to get out?"

"Any way we can," said Decatur without bravado. "But we'll get out, commodore, you may believe that."

"Well, let us hope so." The Old Man picked up his handkerchief and blew his nose with great emphasis. "Damned colds. Damned climate. Damned Bashaw. He wants $120,000 for Bainbridge and his crew. Damned outrage. Don't want to see any more of you people in there. Too expensive. All right. Get along then." He dismissed Decatur and then called him back. "Here. Some port I got from the governor of

Malta. Better have a glass."

Decatur took a glass, and the Old Man surprised him by standing up behind the desk. "To your success, lieutenant. You know how important this is — and you must succeed, no matter the price."

So unusual was this emphasis for the commodore that Decatur was deeply impressed. Like the old Spartans he would come back with his shield or on it — or in modern parlance — he would bring back his crew or he would not come back at all.

The thrill of the coming adventure was now on Decatur. He took his gig back to the *Enterprise*, and the morning was spent turning her over to Lieutenant Dent, the commodore's jack-of-all-trades. By afternoon Decatur and his seventy-four men took boat to the *Intrepid*, where she lay alongside the inner end of the quay, attracting no more attention than a dozen other such craft in the harbor.

Decatur then inspected the little ship. Lawrence and Catalano had done a fine job of making a stout, seaworthy ship of a musty little pirate gunboat. She was painted and trim, and her canvas was new and stout. It seemed a shame that she might have to be fired and sacrificed, but that was war.

In all this, Catalano had made sure that the disguise of the vessel was not penetrated. She was still rigged in the Mediterranean fashion.

The lieutenants, Lawrence, Bainbridge, and Thorn, mustered the volunteer crew, and Decatur stepped forward.

"Men," he said, "we're about to embark on a voyage that is very important to our navy and our country. You know what it is. You also know that there must now be absolute secrecy about our sailing. We sail this evening with the tide. From now until then no one is to go ashore, and no one unauthorized is to board the ship. God be with us."

Decatur then went ashore, to take boat for the *Siren* and confer one last time with Lieutenant Stewart. They met in the cabin of the brig.

"All ready?" asked Stewart.

Decatur nodded.

"You're a lucky dog, Stephen," said his friend.

"I know you wanted to do it," said Decatur, "and I am glad I got there first."

"You'll make it. I know."

"I think we will."

"Now, for sailing. The commodore wants as much secrecy as we can muster. So my crew knows nothing."

"And mine is not only sworn to secrecy but confined to quarters until we sail," said Decatur with a smile.

"So I guess we've taken every precaution. Let's meet at two bells on the day watch tomorrow at sea and take a look at the orders."

"Done," said Decatur, and he got up to leave.

"Oh, one more thing," said Stewart. "This

just came from the Old Man. He told me to deliver it to you by hand."

Decatur broke the seal on the message and opened it.

"Dear Decatur," it said. "Just so nobody will know what you are up to and get the word to the Bashaw, I want you to make a call at the marchesa's palace. Best gossip shop in town. Deliver this message regretting my absence at her party tomorrow night. Let her know you are en route to Malta to rerig the *Intrepid*. That ought to take care of them."

Decatur's pulse quickened. He might have a chance to see Teressa. He had suppressed, very firmly, any thought that this might be the case. But if he called in an hour, there was a chance she would be visiting with the marchesa.

He hurried ashore, and along the cobbles to the palazzo, where he delievered the message as ordered, making quite sure that he engaged the marchesa in the conversation and made his own regrets that he would be unable to attend her fete.

"That is a shame, lieutenant," she said, making a moue. "You are the new celebrity, after the duel. Everyone is talking about it — and wondering why so much fuss was made over what was really a military matter."

The question in her voice was obvious, but Decatur did not rise to the bait. If she suspected, as well she might, that the contessa's name was somehow involved, he was not going to be the

102

one to allay her curiosity.

He was hoping desperately that Teressa might appear here in the morning room. But she did not. And it would have been total betrayal to ask after her, or evince any interest whatsoever. So Decatur was numb and silent. Having carried out his mission, he arose to leave.

In the hallway, he saw her. She was dressed as if she was about to leave, and she espied him at the same moment. A frown of displeasure crossed her face, but she stopped to let him come up with her, and left the house with him, waving away the footman. "No, I will not require the carriage. I am going to the dressmaker, and she is only three blocks down."

Decatur was silent, as they moved toward the corner.

"Why did you do it?" she said in anguish.

"Do what?"

"Maim him."

"I shot to disarm him. After all," he fingered his neck, "he was shooting to kill me."

"That is not what he told me."

"Oh, he has come to call already?"

She ignored the thrust. "He told me he shot over your head and you deliberately aimed at his hand to ruin his career."

"And did he tell you what he had said about yourself?"

"Only that he objected to your attentions to me. And I can understand that. He felt that families of Europe must stick together."

"How do you feel about that?"

"I don't know," she said hurriedly. "He called you a boorish American, intent on destruction. Is that true?"

Decatur was stiff. "You must make your own decisions in such matters, madame."

She became angry. "I think so. I think perhaps Lieutenant Rosmore is right."

"As you say, madame." He touched his hat, and turned. Her route now led off into the center of the city, and his to the quay, and he strode angrily along, his boots clapping loudly on the stones, as she stood, hand to her mouth, looking after him.

12

As Decatur came back aboard the *Intrepid*, just at noon, Bosun's Mate Abby Tyler was standing on deck, holding tightly to a dripping figure.

"What's this?" said Decatur, examining the half-drowned seaman before him.

"It's Stone, sir. Apprentice Seaman Elihu Stone. Swam here from the ship. Said he must talk to you."

"All right, Stone," said Decatur. "What's it all about? If you're trying to desert, you've come to the wrong vessel."

"Not trying to desert, sir," said the youngster. Decatur recalled that he was only nineteen years old. "I want to come on the mission to Tripoli."

"But I already turned you down three days ago," said Decatur. "Look boy. We need strong men on this affair, men who can pull a boat and pull it fast if need be."

"Yessir. I can," said Stone. "Try me."

Abby Tyler spoke up. "He did swim half a mile to get here, sir, and he took an awful risk. Might have been shot in the water as a deserter."

Decatur considered. He was puzzled. "Why do you want to come along, Stone?" he asked.

"They tell me you are a Quaker. I come from Philadelphia, and I know that even killing Berbers is not in your line."

The boy blushed. "I just want to come, sir. I want to see Tripoli."

Abby Tyler broke out — he could not conceal his laughter. "See Tripoli. That's a good one. See Tripoli from the end of a firestick. See Tripoli and burn."

Decatur smiled in spite of himself. "All right. You may come, then. Bosun, send a boat to the *Enterprise* to inform Lieutenant Dent that Apprentice Seaman Stone is not a deserter, but has joined our expeditionary force."

Decatur turned then to the last minute details before sailing. He and Stewart had agreed to move out at two bells on the first dog watch. Stewart was taking a pilot from the *Constitution*, and Decatur had Salvatore Catalano, who now scurried about the deck, making sure he had all his charts and that the throwing lines were new.

A few moments conversation and Decatur had assured himself that Catalano knew precisely what he was about and would carry out his part of the task.

So the afternoon passed, and then it was time. Decatur stood on the main deck, beside Catalano, who took the wheel, for this vessel was not too small to need a wheel. At a signal the lines were cast off, and the *Intrepid* moved out into the tide. Quite separately, the *Siren* hauled anchor and sailed from the middle of the harbor.

To a passerby, it was as though two entirely dissimilar vessels were moving at the same time — one a trim American warship, the other a new, but obviously Mediterranean, ketch, carrying cargo for some island. For Catalano and Decatur were both dressed in the clothes of the Mediterranean seaman: Catalano in a gaudy purple shirt and green trousers, Decatur in gray and white, wearing a headcloth that made him look more like a pirate than a naval officer. The other officers and crew on deck were similarly attired. Having rowed across the harbor, they might have attracted the attention of passersby, or spies, but no ships had gone out that day until the tide changed, and so the chances of the Bashaw having any word of their coming before they arrived were remote.

Expertly, Catalano gave his orders, and Decatur's seamen obeyed, trimming the sheets and putting on sail as told. Decatur stood by the wheel and was silent. There was no need to tell an expert his job. With the ease of experience, Catalano took them out of the tricky narrows and past the rocks, and headed south, down into the bosom of the Mediterranean.

Next morning they met at sea, the *Siren* and the little *Intrepid* well out of sight of land, with no sail in view. Decatur took boat to the larger vessel, clutching his orders, and together they opened their instructions.

"It is my order," wrote Preble, "that you proceed to Tripoli in company with the *Siren*, enter that harbor at night, board the *Philadelphia*, burn her, and make good your retreat in the *Intrepid*, if possible, unless you can make her the means of destroying the enemy's vessels in the harbor by converting her to a fireship for that purpose, and retreating in your boats and those of the *Siren* . . ."

Decatur read these words aloud.

"He doesn't expect much," said Stewart with a grin. "Just go in, burn old *Philly*, then take a gander around the harbor, burn everything else in sight including the Bashaw's castle, and then row out again. Wonder he didn't ask you to swim back."

Decatur laughed. "Those orders are just what I asked for, you know. I only wish he had let me have the chance to sail the *Philadelphia* out."

"It seems to me he's given you quite enough latitude for all the deviltry even you can get into."

"There's one more paragraph. I'm to pay heed to your orders, and if opportunity arises to carry out the obvious portion, to do so. What do your orders say?"

Stewart tore open the envelope, and read quickly. "One thing about the Old Man. He never expects much of his officers. We're to disguise the ship as a merchantman. At least he didn't say how. Then we're to put into the Gulf of Gabes. Five miles east of Jerba there will be a light signal, flashed from a lantern . . ."

"You mean this is at night?"

"Naturally, it's at night. I think the commo-

108

dore would find it too easy otherwise. Ever been to Jerba?"

"Never in my life," said Decatur.

"Then let's hope Catalano or Jourvass has been there. Otherwise we may find ourselves wading from Jerba to Tripoli, with our boats over our shoulders."

"So there's a light," said Decatur.

"We're to meet a spy there. Anatoli is the name. He will give us whatever new information is available about the *Philadelphia* and Tripoli."

Decatur pondered this information. *He* would meet the spy, he and Catalano. That was the oblique reference in the orders obviously. Stewart had neither the complexion nor the rig to do the job, while he, Decatur, could very nicely pass as a Mediterranean citizen, and the clothes in which he was garbed were ridiculous for a navy man, but marvelous cover for a meeting on the coast.

The ships lay hove to half that day, while Stewart set about disguising an American brig of war as a merchantman. First he painted her upper works a dirty brown, and streaked one side of the deckhouses well with soot from the galley fires. The oldest suit of sails was rigged, and the main was slashed and then sewed raggedly, to indicate a hasty repair job. Barrels and bits of lumber were brought on deck, to change the neat lines of a man-of-war, and indicate a sloppy captain. The sheets were allowed to belly and trail in the water, and the anchor chains were twisted and the bow anchor allowed to hang down in an unsightly and almost dangerous fashion. Then, with Lieutenant Stewart doffing his naval uniform hat, and adopting a high blue turtleneck sweater, and his men dressed in mis-matched oddments of their uniforms, and the sails bent just a little awkwardly, the *Siren* would pass very nicely for a merchant brig. Stewart hoisted the British ensign, and Decatur did the same, and they stood in toward the coast of the Tunis plain.

During the afternoon they loafed into the Gulf of Gabes, giving the impression that they were headed for Jerba. But as night fell, they skirted north and east, and approached downwind from the eastern side, moving in toward the shore.

Catalano was indeed familiar with these waters, although never before had he been re-quired to bring a ketch in at night to so unspeci-fied a target as "a point about five miles east of the city." But he assured Decatur that the water here was deep enough for the ketch, that only one set of rocks might threaten them, and that those rocks could be passed safely enough on the eastern side.

Stewart had agreed, reluctantly, that Decatur should go ashore with Catalano, although he had made an effort to take the job himself. But obviously it was to be Decatur's; no other course would have been sensible. So as darkness be-came complete, and the moon was blocked out

110

by clouds, the *Intrepid* was offshore, watching for the signal.

It came — two long blinks from a lantern, followed by three quick short ones. A minute later the signal was repeated. Catalano and Decatur climbed into the boat. Abby Tyler took the tiller, and what appeared to be a crew of ruffianlike sailors from some Mediterranean port began to haul for shore.

The waves lapped along a rocky beach. They put in, guided by more flashes from the lantern. Decatur leaped out of the bow of the boat as she struck the sand, and began hauling her up, but with one hand on the cutlass he was wearing, and an eye peeled for treachery. Catalano was soon out of the boat, and the men pulled her up. Then they got out and stood apparently lounging around the craft. Their eyes were intent on the low lines of the vegetation and rocks around them, watching for any movement.

The light flashed again, and then remained on, a narrow aperture pointing toward them as the bearer came down to the beach.

Ten paces off, a voice spoke. "Americanos?"

"Anatoli?"

"It is I. You are from Syracuse?"

Before them stood a short, very stout man dressed in the costume of a merchant, and wearing a fez. Was he their man? Preble should have given them a sign and countersign, but he had not. Decatur would simply have to trust and watch.

"Yes. Where shall we go to talk?"

"There is a little hut not far from here. We can go there. Tell your men to be silent and lie quietly. For this area is under control of an ally of the Bashaw, my master. The beach is sometimes watched."

They moved slowly to the hut, through sand and then along hard earth, laced with sharp rocks and twisted trees. The path curved in and out, Decatur surmised that it was a smuggler's trail, for it took advantage of every bit of terrain for concealment from the shore.

They came to a rude earthen hut, its mud tiles broken and displaced, door hanging crookedly on its hinge. Puffing hard, their guide doffed his fez and wiped his sweating brow with a silk kerchief, while he placed the lantern on a crude table in the middle of the room.

"I would offer you chairs, but as you can see there are none."

"We have not come for entertainment," said Decatur. "You have some information for us?"

"I hope you will remember Anatoli to your commodore when you return . . ."

"The information?"

"Yes. You know that Bainbridge is being held captive in the Bashaw's castle."

"We know all that."

"But do you know that the *Philadelphia* is about to go to sea?"

"We know all that, too."

The fat little man was crestfallen. "I suppose

112

you know the date?"

"That we do not know."

"It is to be the tenth day of the moon."

"That means ten days from tomorrow," said Catalano. "Tomorrow is the moon's last day; next day begins the new moon."

"You are wise in our ways," said the spy. "You know, too, perhaps, that the Bashaw has recruited his finest men, and Grand Admiral Murad Reis himself will sail the ship on her maiden voyage."

"To Algiers?"

"You know about that, too? What the Americanos do not know, Allah must only suspect." He clasped his hands toward heaven. "Then you must also know that the Dey of Algiers will conclude the treaty the Bashaw wants when the *Philadelphia* puts in to Algiers harbor."

This *was* important. Decatur now saw how vital it was that the *Philadelphia* be destroyed without fail, for in the Bashaw's cause she could prolong this war with the Barbary pirates indefinitely. A coalition between Algiers and Tripoli might break the slender ties that now bound the Emperor of Morocco and other principal leaders along this coast to the European powers. A united North Africa, turned against the West, could force a major struggle, and the United States, just recovering from its own struggle for unity and liberation, was in no position to fight such a war.

The fat little man then withdrew from his shirt

a chart of the Tripoli harbor, which Decatur inspected and handed to Catalano. It showed that the *Philadelphia* had been moved, but her position now was even closer in to the castle and thus more advantageous.

"How many gunboats in the harbor?" asked Decatur.

"There are now twenty," said the spy.

"How are they manned?"

"With the pick of the Bashaw's seamen and fighters."

"At night?"

"Day and night."

"And the *Philadelphia*?"

"A full crew of seamen. But the fighters are not yet aboard."

That was something to be thankful for. Decatur and Catalano pored over the chart of the harbor, while Anatoli stood nervously by them holding the lantern. Suddenly he started.

"A noise," he whispered. He doused the lamp. They all stood quiet. Indeed, there had been a noise, the sound of movement in the sandy brush outside, not close, but not far away.

Decatur dropped to his knees and crept to the doorway, shutting his eyes tight to accustom them to the darkness outside the hut. Two hundred yards away, against the light from the seaward side, he saw a flutter of motion, then another.

"Someone's coming," he said.

"Sheikh Anali's men, I fear," said the little

merchant. "We must be off. I go by the land trail back to the city. You had best come with me. I shall try to hide you."

Decatur considered. The men he had seen were between himself and the boat. Had they seen and overpowered Tyler and the others? He had heard no signs of struggle, and it most certainly would have involved a struggle, unless they had crept up so silently as to surround, snatch, and garrote the men. Knowing Abby Tyler, Decatur did not believe this could have occurred. Tyler must have seen them, and somehow was lying low, waiting.

"No," he said. "We must act. It would be more dangerous for us to go to Jerba than to make our escape here."

"They are Berbers," said the spy.

He had said everything, as Catalano well knew, and as Decatur had begun to learn. To be captured by Berbers, particularly if one was an American, was to invite torture and death. Especially right now, when the Bashaw and the other chieftains were not finding it easy to blackmail the United States with the captives on hand, they were eager to sacrifice a few lives to prove a point.

The spy needed little more urging. With an agility quite belied by his form, he crept through the door, around in back of the hut, and was gone, making almost no noise.

Decatur and Catalano lay silent for a moment. Then they heard the sounds of men moving, but this time the noise was much closer. They could not be much more than a hundred yards away.

Decatur felt for his weapons. He had his pistol, but that meant only one charge. He had the cutlass he had brought with him, not as good a weapon for a swordsman as his long sword, but good enough for close fighting. Catalano was wearing a scimitar of the Turkish variety on his right side and a long poniard at his left. They were as well armed as they could expect to be. They could assume that the men coming would be armed with guns, swords and daggers. How many of them were there?

The answer to that question would have to wait a little.

Decatur whispered to Catalano, then took the lantern up, put it on the table, and looked at the pilot. He was at the door of the hut. Decatur opened the door of the dark lantern, so the rays fell on the back wall of the hut. From outside it would appear that a light was being shielded, that a person or persons were inside. And as he opened the door, and the light shone forth, he dropped to the floor, and followed Catalano outside.

The hut was on a little rocky hill, and a long ridge twisted sharply down to the sea. The rocks were loose and sliding, but at the bottom was a narrow ravine, which could bring them out on the beach, if they were lucky. The problem was to cross down into the ravine without betraying themselves, and Decatur knew that it could not be done without disturbing the loose rock, creating as much noise as a charging bull.

They must somehow trick the Berbers into believing they were going in another direction or that they were dead.

Decatur whispered to Catalano again, and the other nodded. He stood for a moment, careful not to silhouette himself, and shouted in Arabic.

"Who comes?"

Silence. Then a noise, a rustling, like the movement of many men.

"We've got to get away from the hut," said Decatur. On his belly he began worming his way along the top of the ridge, down toward the sea. The danger was that at any moment a man of the rear guard of the enemy force would meet him eye to eye along the ridge.

But the Berbers were on the other side, coming from the landward now. They did not choose to fan out so far as to try to cross the ravine. For they, too, would face the problem of making too much noise. Not knowing what kind of force they were up against, they would assume that whoever was there would have guns, too.

Decatur had one shot. It must be made to serve him well.

Catalano hailed again. This time a voice came in reply.

"Who are you interlopers? This is the domain of the great Sheikh Abd Ali Abd Akhbar Anali, may his ancestors lie in heaven. Come and show yourselves."

Catalano looked at Decatur. The lieutenant picked up a stone, and threw it so that it struck the side of the hut. A figure showed itself not ten yards from the entrance. Decatur fired. There was a cry, and then a swift return of fire from a dozen guns, but aimed off to the right of the hut, at right angles to Decatur and the pilot.

Then came a rapid exchange of talk in Arabic.

"You've hit one of them in the arm," said Catalano. "Not serious. But they now vow that they will kill the dogs that dared fire on the sheikh's men."

"All right, if they can," said Decatur. "At least they'll be careful to stay out of gun range. And that's what we had to have. What kind of actor are you?"

"Actor?"

Decatur hurried on. "Hail them again. Provoke fire. Then when a shot is fired I shall make a noise like a dying man, and we will get down into the ravine. No time to stop. Keep going, for God's sake, once we get started."

Catalano cried out again, taunting the sheikh's men in the name of Shaitan, and shots rang out. Decatur screamed, and then moaned. The two hurled themselves down the gulley, rattling the stones as they went. At the bottom they found a tiny rivulet, wet enough. This was winter. They began crawling, slipping, and running toward the sea. Above they could hear the sounds of men crashing through the brush and searching along the sides of the ravine.

Ten minutes went by. Decatur's hands were scratched and bleeding. He had cut his face on a sharp outcrop of rock, and he assumed that Catalano was in no better shape. They had perhaps two hundred yards' lead on their pursuers, who were hampered by the need to search both sides as they came down the ravine. But if Decatur and Catalano did not reach the beach soon, they would exhaust their strength.

Then, around one last bend in the gulley, they pulled out onto a shelf, and ten feet below was the beach, with a little waterfall from the rivulet dropping onto stone and splashing.

Decatur led Catalano in jumping down, into the pool below. He followed the water out into the surf, turned east toward their boat, and ran a hundred yards before he headed back to the hard wet sand.

"That should stop them for a few minutes," he said. "But they will be on the beach soon enough, and they will be after us. Run."

They ran down the beach, panting and fighting the stabbing pains of exhaustion that lanced their lungs.

It was half a mile by beach to the boat, and as they came up, panting so hard they could scarcely speak, Abby Tyler sensed that they were hotly followed, and he had the men pushing the boat into the water.

"Three men with muskets," Decatur panted. "Wait till you see them, then let them have a volley."

"Aye, aye, sir." No sooner said than done. Tyler took a gun himself. Decatur and Catalano used their reserves of strength to help push the boat into the surf.

"Here they come, sir."

"Then fire, and let's move."

The muskets rang out, the flashes bright in the darkness, and the line of men who could be seen dimly moving toward them stopped short. Decatur grabbed Abby Tyler and hustled into the boat, pushed the others, and shoved the boat off, just as with a wailing cry the men behind began to charge forward, brandishing swords. A few knelt to fire their weapons, and the balls came by, close, but not hitting anyone. The boat was in the surf, and then through it, and the fresh oarsmen pulled hard to get out to sea and to the safety of the *Intrepid*, lying just a few cables off the shore.

The further they moved out, the better organized the enemy on shore became, and at the last, a whole series of shots rang out. But they fell short, for Berber powder was not designed for long-range fighting. The men in the boat moved alongside the ketch, and eager hands helped them up. Decatur had scarcely gained the deck when the boat was hoisted in, and he gave orders to move out to sea. He wished to share his news with Stewart. It was time to get at the *Philadelphia*. There was not an hour to lose.

13

The two captains conferred in early morning.
Stewart quite agreed that no time could be lost,
lest the Tripoli pirates bring the *Philadelphia* out
and vastly complicate the whole Barbary war. The
day watch had not ended before they were heading for the target as fast as the little ketch would
sail. The *Siren* was a good sailor in the open sea,
and Decatur saw that Stewart had to keep his canvas trimmed lest he run away from his charge. Yet
on the other hand, the disparate sailing strengths
of the two vessels was an advantage. Stewart liter-
ally ran rings around them, and to the casual ob-
server, there was no relationship between the
common Mediterranean ketch, flying its British
flag, and the bigger merchant brig, except that
they flew the same ensign.

To get the best out of the *Intrepid*, Decatur
had rigged her with a tiny top on the mainmast,
above which rose the topmast, and he had gone
one further to give her a tiny topgallant mast.
Since the Mediterranean ketches were rigged
according to the preference of their owners, this
inspired no particular comment except that the
little ship looked, and was, top-heavy when she

was fully clothed in sail and drawing hard.

Decatur knew it, but felt the need for speed in this endeavor. The strain was tremendous on these upper spars, and as the *Intrepid* reached for the Tripoli shore, she heeled heavily in the freshening wind, and the pressure on the cross trees and the upper running rigging was enormous.

Able-bodied Seaman Merchant Smith was main topman on the evening watch, and just after three bells, he saw the furry slapping of a line that indicated a lashing had come undone. Although the ship was heeling briskly over, he began climbing the ratlines to secure the piece.

As he left the top and moved upward, a sudden gusty squall slapped across the *Intrepid* and turned her halfway around. Only the sharp eye and quick reaction of the man at the wheel kept her from jibing, which might well have dismasted her, and put an end to the *Philadelphia* adventure altogether.

Decatur could bless his luck, and the skill of his helmsman, but Seaman Smith was not so lucky. He reached one bronzed hand for the shroud, missed as the ship lurched, and fell thirty feet to the deck, lighting on an iron stanchion with the full force of his left shoulder. His head thunked the deck with a sound that caused Abby Tyler to look up from his task of testing the anchor chain housing. He saw Smith lying in a most unnatural position and ran to him, picking up the slender form of the man — he was only twenty, scarcely more than a boy. Smith groaned.

122

"My arm, bosun. It must be broken."

Tyler nodded, and carried him below, where Surgeon Heerman had already been called into the cabin, stump of a cigar clenched between his teeth. The surgeon grimaced as he looked at the bleeding arm. Gently, he explored the fracture, and Decatur, who had come at the call, saw a splintered piece of white bone sticking through.

The surgeon beckoned him outside, and as they stood on deck he spoke softly. "I'll have to take that arm off," he said. "Both bone and sinews are torn to bits. If I don't he's sure to develop gas poisoning and die."

Decatur frowned. Smith was one of his most trusted men and now he would be lost to the service. But there was no other course. He nodded, and they returned to the little cabin, where the injured seaman lay on the table, head rolling from side to side in pain.

"Get him a good big tot of rum," said Surgeon Heerman. "I might as well tell you, boy. I can't save your arm. But I can save your life and that I am going to do. It's going to hurt, and you're going to howl. But remember, you *will* pull through. "

From the galley Cronky brought a basin of hot water, and the surgeon laid out his instruments. Decatur handed the boy the rum, and supported his head as he drank it down in a gulp. Heerman gave Smith a smooth piece of black ebony. "When it starts to hurt, bite on this. It will help."

The surgeon then set to work, cutting first the

ragged flesh away from the bone, and tying off the bleeders. Smith grimaced and his teeth clamped down on the block of wood.

Tyler and Midshipman Macdonough held Smith by shoulders and chest as he squirmed involuntarily, and Midshipman Morris held his feet. Heerman picked up his bone saw.

"Gently now boys," he said. "Gently." And Decatur shuddered as the saw grated on the bone.

Smith gave a cry, and then the block of wood fell to the floor.

"Thank God, he's fainted," said the surgeon. "Now let me be quick with it." He sawed for a moment, then picked up the scalpel and severed the twisted, hanging arm from the shoulder.

"Bring the iron," he directed. Cronky came from the galley bearing a red hot poker, and the surgeon passed it along the stump, searing the red flesh until the bleeding stopped. The stink of burning filled the cabin until Decatur thought he would be sick and rushed outside to gulp in clean sea air.

When he returned, Heerman was calmly mopping up the blood on the table. "There," the surgeon said. "With a little luck he'll be all right now. Move him to a bunk before he wakes up."

The accident and the memory of the operation hung a cloud over the ship, and men passing each other on deck looked sternly or sadly at one another. How many more of them would feel the bite of the surgeon's knife, or worse, would feel nothing at all, before this adventure was over?

But in an hour, the misery of Seaman Smith was forgotten, for the forward lookout shouted, "Land!" and every eye turned toward the spit ahead that guarded the harbor of Tripoli.

The wind was bearing from the northeast, and if it held till evening, the ships would have a simple reach to sail to move into the harbor. As for the afternoon, the sun shone down, and it was a most pleasant day for early February. Pilot Catalano loafed at the wheel, keeping an eye out aft, for a mile astern, and tacking back and forth was the *Siren*, keeping up the pretense of placidity, and paying no apparent attention to the Maltese ketch.

Night fell, and Catalano turned the *Intrepid* toward the harbor. The tide was flowing in; in two hours it would begin to ebb, and this would be just right for the work ahead. Come in with one tide, go out with the next.

But as the *Intrepid* neared the harbor, black clouds rose from the east and moved over the ship. The wind suddenly increased and the rain began pelting the little craft, damping her sails in a minute.

Catalano kept a straight course, straining at the wheel to keep the compass lined up. Suddenly, however, he spun the wheel, and the *Intrepid* headed up into the wind, and then off on a starboard tack.

Decatur had been below, checking men and

weapons, and making sure that each of his officers knew, letter perfect, his part of the plan. With the shift in motion he came on deck and made his way aft to look inquiringly at the pilot.

"You've headed up," he said. "Why the change?"

"I don't like this weather, lieutenant," said Pilot Catalano. "One stretch between the rocks, just before you get into harbor, is extremely treacherous. One never goes in when there is a storm like this."

Decatur's eyebrows narrowed. "How long will it be?" he asked.

The pilot shrugged. "These winter storms. No one can say. Perhaps in an hour it will be clear and we can move in. Perhaps it will be a day or more."

Glumly, Decatur nodded. His men were keyed up for the action, and delay would bring a serious drop in morale. Moreover, he had no way of knowing what had happened to the spy Anatoli. What if the sheikh's men had captured him. A few touches of the bastinado, and Decatur was sure the whole plan would be revealed. That would be the end of it. This undertaking depended entirely on the element of surprise. If the Bashaw gained the slightest notion that an effort on the *Philadelphia* was in progress it would be simple enough to so surround her with gunboats and to plant so many men aboard her that the assault must surely fail.

An hour passed, and the wind grew no more

favorable. Catalano moved westward, hoping that in the lee of the reefs it might prove easier, but it was not.

"You're sure," said Decatur anxiously, "that there is no chance of going in."

"I do not say that, lieutenant," said Catalano. "I said that no captain who sails this port would risk his vessel in such an enterprise."

"Nor will I, then," said Decatur. It would be foolhardy to waste the lives of these men, or to have them run the danger of capture with so little margin for success. "We shall wait."

Another hour passed, and again Decatur came to the wheel.

"Let's make sure," he said. "I'm detailing Midshipman Morris to take you and a boat crew over to the entrance to take a good look."

So a boat was put over the side, with some difficulty, in the punishing sea, and two men took their places at the oars, wrapping rags around the locks so they would not creak. Morris sat in the sternsheets, and the pilot moved into the bow. The boat headed through the sheets of rain toward the harbor entrance. In half an hour it returned.

"No luck," said Midshipman Morris. "We went almost up to the rocks. The sea is breaking at least ten feet high over them. And the wind was shifting again, we'd never be able to sail out in the teeth of it."

Catalano's wisdom was confirmed in less than an hour. The wind rose to gale proportions, shrieking and tearing at the rigging and the sails, and Decatur ordered the pilot to take the ketch back out into the open sea for safety.

Late that night the wind seemed to diminish, and the *Intrepid* turned back toward Tripoli. This time, Decatur ordered the ship anchored; that would draw no attention, any watcher from shore who happened to catch a glimpse of the ketch would assume that the captain was a wise soul who was waiting out the tempest before coming into port. Once again Catalano and Morris stepped into the little boat, and sailed toward the reef line, but this time, before they had been gone fifteen minutes, the storm broke again with renewed fury upon the ketch, and she tossed dreadfully in the seas, creaking and banging against the anchor chain.

Decatur stood in the bow, searching for signs of his boat, and when it came, he saw that it was bobbing like a cork in the frightening waves. Somehow the seamen managed to bring the boat alongside the *Intrepid* on the lee, but as the men scurried and scampered up the Jacob's ladder thrown down to them, the boat and ship turned in the wind, and the boat began pounding against the side of the ketch. Morris had grasped the rope ladder, and was pulling himself up, when the gunwale splintered, the side stove in, and before he was on the deck, the boat was torn away and hurled, half sinking, from the *Intrepid*.

Decatur looked out to sea, then toward the land, and found the sky so threatening and the waves so high that he knew there would be no chance for them until the storm had passed, so the *Intrepid* turned again and ran before the storm trying to escape to the northward.

14

What had been a fresh gale in the evening began to strengthen, and the clouds unleashed the full wet fury of the heavens. The rain pelted down, and as it was caught by the wind it was driven like shot against the ship and the men who manned her; when it struck Decatur's face it had the sting of sleet. The glass dropped fast, which meant a heavy storm, and by midnight the barometer's reading was fully confirmed. The waves rose high above the ship. Had she been riding in the trough, her decks would constantly have been awash.

But early on, since Catalano predicted at least a storm and perhaps even a hurricane — although hurricanes were rare in Mediterranean waters — Decatur had ordered the battening down of the ketch. The mainsail was tightly reefed, and finally brought down altogether; the staysails were hauled down or reefed until only a small triangle carried the ship to help prevent her making leeway. She sailed on the jib, and that was quite enough to keep her headed up, just off the wind, so she would not roll and dip into the troughs. There was no question of getting anywhere. For a time Catalano had spoken of running for Malta, but that plan had been given up in mid evening, as the storm grew worse. Midnight brought her changing with the wind, fighting for survival.

Last Decatur had seen of the *Siren*, she was lying, anchored, off the Tripoli roads, waiting for Decatur to go in and do his job. Then the storm had blown the *Intrepid* away, and the *Siren* was slow to follow, delayed in getting her anchor up, although Decatur did not know it then. So the little ketch fought her battle alone, and as the wind came, she was blown steadily southeastward, toward the Gulf of Sidra.

In Syracuse, the men of the American squadron had been living off the land; the local chandlers brought fresh provisions every day. They had green vegetables, and oranges, and fresh bread from the bakeries. Local farmers carted in chickens and pigs and even fresh beef. But a ship at sea had no place to store more than three or four days' supply of fresh provisions, and so when the *Intrepid* was fitted out, even though Decatur firmly expected he would be in and out of port within a week, he had taken the precaution of laying in the sailors' standbys, salt beef and barrels of hardtack.

On the second day of the storm, Cronky, the cook, noted that his provisions of fresh food had deteriorated, the vegetables were slimy, the meat gone bad. So he ordered his scullion boys to throw the trash overboard, and called for a cask of salt beef. The stoves in the galley were alight, and with clamps and a heavy hand he could hold his fortress together and get out a meal even though the deck was canting thirty degrees beneath him. The two boys, Ezra Bean and Obadiah Strong, came puffing up from the hold, wrestling the hundred-pound barrel, and deposited it on end at the cook's feet.

"There," he said. "Take a blow. I'll just take the top off this now, and quick as a flying fish we'll have a gullion going."

So Cronky picked up his cleaver and prized off the lid of the barrel, leaned forward, and stepped back, with a roar of rage.

"Rotten, by God," he shouted. "Those dirty seaslugs from Georgetown have sent us rotten meat. Young Bean, you go out and hail the captain. I want him to smell this."

The boy ran from the galley to the wheel, where he found Decatur spelling Catalano with the quartermaster.

"Sir, the cook wants you right away."

Decatur did not question him. Cronky would not have called on the captain were it not for some serious problem. So he headed forward, and bracing himself and hauling hand over hand on the lifelines, he made his way to the galley, arriving there drenched, but that was to be expected.

"Look here lieutenant," was Cronky's greeting. "Stick your head in this mess."

Decatur put his nose over the cask, and the putrid odor of rotting meat assailed him.

"Are they all like this?" he asked.

"Don't know. This is the first I tried."

"Bring up another."

So the boys went below again and brought up another cask of meat, but it was as putrid as the first.

Decatur got down on hands and knees and examined the cask from one end to the other, as Cronky muttered about the lying bastards who had tried to poison honest sailors off fighting their wars for them.

"Don't blame the provisioner, cook," Decatur said. "It's the barrelmaker you want to take a stave to. Look at this." And he showed how the hoops had worked loose and let the pickle brine run out from the casks before they could set the meat.

"Throw the rotten meat overboard," he said. "Try every cask and then report to me."

So ten casks of meat were brought up and tried, one by one, and the whole of them were rotten. When Surgeon Heerman heard, he was solemn and quiet, for he knew better than the others what a diet of hardtack and nothing but hardtack could do to a crew in a week.

"We have to live with it," said Decatur. "This blow ought to end in a day or so, then we can get in and be in port in five days."

But Decatur was an optimist, and the Mediterranean was not listening as he spoke. The storm did abate to a gale, but the gale persisted day after day, and although the *Intrepid* was headed up northwestward, and never deviated, every hour saw her blown further and further southeast.

Three days went by. Around noon on the third day the wind slackened, and for a moment Decatur thought he caught a glimpse of the sun, but it was only that one tantalizing moment, for half an hour later the wind had shifted three points but was blowing as hard as ever, and the scud was driving in their faces.

The days were bad enough, but the nights were dreadful. In daylight even the men off watch could be on deck or crouched in small corners of the upper works. But by night there was nowhere to go but to the pitifully small quarters. From sternpost to jib boom the ketch was soaked in sea water and rain, the bilges were running with fresh flow, and the pumps never stopped although she was not stove or even leaking badly. Below, the men jammed together, more than sixty in the forecastle, occupying space that had been intended for a dozen sailors, overflowing down into the cargo hold. When he was not at the wheel, Pilot Catalano slept on a platform erected atop the water casks. Sleep was scarcely the word for it, Decatur thought when he saw the place. The platform was nothing more than a narrow board shelf, so close to the main deck that Catalano could not sit up without striking his head on the decking. He shared this space with the six midshipmen. Opposite, to port, eight marines had similar accommodations. It would be a wonder, Decatur told himself, if any of them got an hour's sleep in twenty-four.

But Decatur's lot was not much better. He, his three other lieutenants, and Surgeon Heerman occupied the one small cabin, and with the injury of Smith, they had made room for him. It had been no good taking him forward — there simply was not enough room. So the result was that none of the men in the cabin got much rest even when they tried.

At the end of four days they were red-eyed and half hysterical. Any joke brought laughter of a force that defied the gale roaring over them. They munched on hardtack, swallowed stiffly, and gulped down fresh water. Lieutenant Thorn had tried to shave on the second day — he was the most careful of all of them about his appearance — but had cut his cheek with the razor, and had the good sense to stop before he slashed his throat. By the fourth day he was as ragged as any of them, but by the fifth, they might have entered the lowest dive in Syracuse port and not have attracted a penny's worth of attention, such a raunchy crew were the gentlemen of the after cabin.

Surprisingly enough, the wetting, the salt water, the chill, seemed to alleviate Seaman Smith's fever. Though he had shown optimism, Surgeon Heerman had not really held much hope for the boy. He knew what happened to amputees at sea. Too often it was gangrene and death. But for reasons he did not understand Smith passed the crisis on the third night and began to mend. The stump scabbed over, and there was no pus. He seemed to know, too, and was the most cheerful man in the cabin, refusing help whenever he could take care of himself, and even trying to get up, before he was ordered back on his bunk by Decatur.

On the sixth day, Decatur came on deck with the report of a sail in sight. The clouds had lifted enough that there was a horizon once again, although not much of one, and only to the north of them. But there, a few hundred cables away, was a ship. Training his glass, Decatur quickly recognized the *Siren*. So she had been blown along with them. She had suffered more than the *Intrepid*, he saw through the glass. Her fore skysail was gone, ripped away by the wind. Tatters still hung there, for Stewart was not such a fool as to send men aloft in the weather they had been experiencing. Two of her port boats were stove, as Decatur could see, and a long segment of her rail was missing. But she rode soundly, and did not seem to be in distress.

For two more days the storm blew on. The danger to the *Intrepid* grew every hour. The seams of the vessel lost their oakum, and she began to leak badly, so that the pumps did not seem able to keep up. She was sluggish, and wanted to come up to port. The seas smashed over her, and she shuddered, but instead of bouncing up as she had in the first days, she came back like a tired old dog. In truth, as Decatur knew, a few more days of this and they were almost certain to founder. The *Intrepid* was an inter-island ketch, not made for such rough work as this; her builders had never expected her to spend a week at sea fighting a storm.

The loosening of the seams brought out the worst in the *Intrepid.* The rats grew frantic and raced across the bodies of the men in the hold, trying to find some shelter from the wet. The sailors who had manned the ship when she was the *Mastico* seemed to have collected every variety of vermin known to the wide Mediterranean, and the soaking of the spaces below decks made them seek warmth and comfort, which they found in the hair and bodies of officers and men. Below, the sailors and marines found their only exercise in calisthenics, and their only amusement in cracking lice. And as the week wore on, the effects of torpor, bad food, and boredom were taking their toll on the morale of the crew.

Decatur became aware of this when he made his morning tour on the seventh day. He came down the hatchway in a moment, his usual way, and as he glanced at the marines, huddled on their shelf, he sensed from their attitude of watchful silence that he had interrupted a conversation.

He bent and walked to a point three feet from the shelf.

"All right," he said. "Spit it out. What's the scuttlebutt?"

"What do you mean, lieutenant?" asked Corporal Sturdevant innocently. "We were just sitting here cracking bugs."

"Don't try to fool the lieutenant," said Private Ross. "You're right, sir, there is some scuttlebutt."

Decatur looked his question.

"Well, you see, sir," said Sturdevant apologetically, to atone for his attempt at dissimulation, "a lot of the men don't think we're going to make it. They figure the Ayrabs must have seen us when we were fooling around outside the harbor."

Decatur listened, appalled. The success or failure of the whole venture depended on the kind of enthusiasm he had met in the very beginning. Hesitation, doubt, these were his deadly enemies. A moment's delay in firing a charge or planting a fire bomb could mean the end of the gang of them.

Irritation flashed through him.

"You want to go back to Syracuse, then, eh? Well, if that's what you want, we'll take the ship back; and I'll report to the commodore that it was impossible for the men of the *Enterprise* to do the task. If that's what you want men, that's what you're going to get."

He turned on his heel and left the compartment, with a vigor he did not feel.

An hour went by, an hour in which Decatur cursed himself for a fool a dozen times. He and his mouth. He could not take the ship back to Syracuse, unless he wished to leave the navy. Another would have ordered a flogging of the man who started the rumor — if he could find him, and if he could not find the culprit then somebody would have been flogged to give the rest of them a lesson. To lay his commission on the line was a fool's move, and he deserved to be cashiered if it came to that.

But as he stood amidships, gazing upward and cursing the storm that seemed to be unending, he heard a cough from right beside him, and turning, found Corporal Sturdevant, hat in hand, looking most disconsolate.

"Sir," said the corporal, shouting to make himself heard, and hanging onto the stanchion beside him for support as the wind buffeted the ketch. "I've been talking down below. It's just the food, sir, and the damned storm. Nobody wants to quit, sir. If you say we'll make it, we'll make it."

Decatur's eyes shone, and he had to restrain himself from clapping Sturdevant on the back.

"Aye, aye," he said, in his most offhand voice. "Then we'll proceed as planned. No more rumors."

The corporal turned to go. Decatur called after him then.

"And Sturdevant," he said, smiling as the man turned back, "thank you."

The answering grin from the marine was a promise, Decatur knew, that there would be no more trouble aboard the *Intrepid* on this trip.

15

As if the gods of the sea were in league with the seamen below the deck of the *Intrepid*, an hour after the conversation with Corporal Sturdevant, the sky seemed less leaden, the color of the water less muddy green, the spray less stinging in Decatur's face. And by the change of the watch, he could sense a very definite lowering of the wind, and a switch in its direction. Two hours later the waves had subsided, and the little ketch had stopped its dreadful pitching. By nightfall the sea was calm, and as if to remind the sailors of their insignificance in the world scheme, the sun set in a blaze of purple and golden glory that gave the lie to any thought at all of storm.

That night the two ships drew close together and Decatur took his boat to the *Siren* to confer with Stewart. He found his friend with his arm in a sling.

"What happened?" asked Decatur, as they moved into the commander's cabin.

"I was smashed against the windlass when we were trying to get the anchor up," said Stewart. "We really should have gone in that night. It would have saved the ship a lot of trouble."

"And me," said Decatur, scratching vigorously.

"You," laughed the other. "You're getting into stride now. Back home they'd put you on the stage. The Pirate of Malta. How's that for a name?"

Looking into Stewart's shaving mirror, Decatur got an inkling of what his friend meant. Back at him stared a frightening visage, a scrabbly beard covering a dark and dirt-stained face, turban half askew and filthy with grease, shirt tattered on one shoulder and black with tar on the other.

"Well, at least we're right for the task," Decatur laughed. And laughter over, they sat down to renew their plan.

Decatur would lead and the other ship would follow as before. The break in the *Siren*'s rail and the tattered canvas would only help to strengthen their cover story that they were British traders looking for shelter and repairs after the storm. The watchword for the action would be *Philadelphia*. They would head to Tripoli next morning, and make the city by afternoon.

Decatur returned to the ketch, and ordered Catalano to set a course for Tripoli once more. They sailed away, and the *Siren* made ready to dawdle a while before following them, so that there would be no chance of another vessel putting two and two together and getting the right answer.

In the morning, *Intrepid* was alone, which

Decatur found comfortable enough. The sky was as bright as if the word *storm* was quite foreign to Mediterranean waters, the gulls were wheeling about the ship, calling for food, and a school of porpoises joined them for an hour, leaping and tumbling beneath the bow like children in the water.

Late afternoon came, and with it Decatur's expectation that they would soon be joined by the *Siren*. Catalano pointed out that the tide would be just right two hours after dark. The moon would be in its first quarter, and they would have their opportunity. The weather would be clear and the seas quiet, both of which had been denied them just a week earlier.

But as darkness fell, there was still no sign of the *Siren*, and Decatur fretted. He could make the attempt, but his orders called for him to act in concert with the other ship. The commodore liked to have his orders obeyed. There was no reason to believe that anything could have happened to Stewart; he had spoken with him just twenty-four hours earlier. So he would wait, chafing though his young bloods might be, and eager as he was himself.

Morning came, another sunny, bright winter's day, but still no sign of the *Siren*. The hours moved along in the glass, and still nothing. Suddenly Decatur heard Catalano curse.

"There is trouble, signor," said the pilot, pointing off on the horizon, a few points west of the Tripoli shore.

At first it was just a daub on the seascape, then it became a sail, and finally it showed as a ketch remarkably similar to their own, heading in along the shore line for the city that lay between them.

"I sensed it," said Catalano gloomily. "It is Ettore Martini, and the ship he sails is our sister. They were built in the same yard, and Martini knows this ketch as well as he knows his own."

"And Martini's allegiances?"

"His father was a Sicilian. His mother an Egyptian dancing girl. He has been making his living on the sea, like I myself, since he was a boy. Allegiances? To men like Martini, allegiances are something for people of big powers."

"But yourself?"

"I was lucky. I call Malta home. The British say they own Malta. So I say the British own me."

Decatur was thoughtful. "You are sure he will recognize us?"

"As sure as I know that the fish will eat today."

"Then we must intercept him."

"And?"

Decatur refused to commit himself. "That we will have to decide when we talk to your friend. Right now, let us go and take him before he gets inside the reef."

So the *Intrepid* bent on every bit of sail, the American crewmen moved swiftly when they knew there was an emergency. Decatur was careful not to show more than a dozen men on deck — the little ship could have been sailed by half a dozen easily, but a dozen would seem foolish only, not menacing.

"It will not be hard," said Catalano. "He will be curious as to why we have changed the color, why we have new sails. He has not been to Sicily recently, and I would not think he has heard of our change of nationality, the *Mastico*'s and mine."

"Yours?"

"Why, of course," smiled the Maltese. "I am an American sailor now."

Decatur was not cheered by Catalano's joke, for he recalled only too well that the pilot had whiled away hours during the storm telling bad Maltese jokes, mostly about his British protectors.

But whatever he could do, Catalano could coax the best out of the ketch, and it was not half an hour before they overhauled the other vessel, and Decatur and the pilot put off in a boat to interpose themselves before she could turn into the channel that led to Tripoli harbor.

They boarded, Catalano in the lead, hailing his friend and shouting out the news that he had taken over the *Mastico* and changed her name.

As they came on deck, they were greeted by a heavy-set man in clothes not unlike their own, although much cleaner. He also sported an enormous handlebar mustache.

Decatur was introduced as an American friend. But that was before the remainder of the

144

boat crew clambered aboard, and ranged themselves around the lieutenant and his companions.

Then Decatur spoke up.

"I am sorry Signor Martini — but I am a lieutenant in the United States Navy. Signor Catalano is under my orders, and I must now ask you to place yourself there, too."

A shadow of anger crossed the face of the burly man, and his hand moved toward his sword.

"For what purpose, signor?"

"For the purpose of aiding my mission, which is the destruction of the frigate *Philadelphia* in Tripoli harbor."

"You mean to make war on the Bashaw."

"That is right." Decatur was ready, he nodded meaningfully at his men. There were eight of them, and perhaps a dozen in Martini's crew. They would have to move fast to take them, without creating a fuss that someone on shore was sure to see.

But Martini's hand dropped away from the sash, and he began shaking with suppressed laughter. Then tears came to his eyes. "You mean you fear that I would help the Bashaw?"

"We do not know your feelings."

The big captain spit, the globule carrying out over the lee of the ship. "That is what I think of the Bashaw. Has not Catalano a tale of his own? With me it was a girl — I wanted her — the Bashaw wanted her. He got the girl. I got these."

He raised his shirt and showed white scars across his back, the marks of what looked like a flaying lashing.

Martini looked around at his crew, *"Basta,"* he shouted. "Enough. Get back to your duties." He turned and said confidentially to Decatur, "Not one of them would lift a finger to save a sailor from *that* harbor." He spat again toward Tripoli. "And I wager that every man would have a story like my own or Salvatore's to tell you of the treachery of those people. No my friend. You can put me under any orders you want until you finish this mission. Then of course . . ." and his thumb rubbed forefinger and middle finger in a gesture Decatur had come to know very well.

"What we need," said Decatur, "is support outside the harbor while we make our entrance."

He proceeded then, after a reassuring glance from Catalano, to outline his basic plan to the Sicilian captain, who nodded vigorously and smiled widely in appreciation of what was to come.

"Signor," said the big man, "my ship and our lives are at your service. If you succeed, you and your brave men, you will have torn the very sinews from the Bashaw's arms."

With this assurance, Decatur's hopes once again rose that he might complete the mission and return safely. For his doubts had begun to grow. If they were unable to get in that night, the danger would be increased mightily. Someone was going to see the ketch standing off the harbor and remember having seen it a week before, on the day the storm began. That much could be explained easily enough. But if the *Intrepid* had to hang around the entrance for another day, waiting for the *Siren,* then indeed it would be a stupid defender inside who would not begin to suspect that the little ship was up to no good.

With a sense of urgency, Decatur took his men back to the *Intrepid,* and once aboard called a meeting of his officers. When the whole dozen had assembled in the crowded cabin, he spoke.

"Tonight must be the night," he said.

Grave faces and nods of assurance showed him that they were with him — that the long hard days of inactivity had not sapped their resolve.

"A good thing," said Lieutenant Bainbridge, scratching himself vigorously. "I cannot tell you how eager I am to get back to the squadron and get a bath."

"And something to eat," added Midshipman Morris, whose appetite had been a source of admiration on the lower decks of the *Constitution.*

Decatur grinned at them. Such talk was the normal conversation of healthy young men, not that of disaffected sailors on a disagreeable job.

"Then, let's get ready," he said briskly, and they were dismissed.

As the afternoon wore away, Decatur occasionally scanned the horizon to the southeast, whence the *Siren* should appear, had nothing gone awry with her. But no luck. He was content anyway. Outside there would be the other ketch, and if need be they could swim to her, and still have a fair chance of escaping any pursuit. Considering his orders, he hoped Stewart would arrive by nightfall, but considering the wind, he dared wait no longer. Catalano said that by midnight the wind might well be dead, and the harbor deadly calm as a result of it — that was not unusual in this latitude in winter. Then, if he got in, he might not be able to reach the *Philadelphia.* And if he got that far, he might not be able to get back out again in time.

So it was this night or never as far as the *Intrepid* was concerned, and it could not be never. If he went home to Syracuse without at least having made the attempt, the commodore would never again employ him on a mission that required valor. Such had never been said, but Decatur knew the Old Man, and what he expected. Everything he knew added up to the same answer.

As dusk came down, the wind grew lighter, and this state of affairs brought a new anxiety. What if the wind died before dark? The plan was to move in under cover of the blackness of night, but the plan might miscarry.

Decatur sought Catalano, who could offer no promises, and a look at the shiver of the mainsail told him what he needed to know.

There was an answer. "Mr. Lawrence," he

148

called, and when the first lieutenant came to him he pointed astern. "Break out the buckets, port and starboard, and fashion some sea anchors. Two port and two starboard. Tow them well astern. Then tell Mr. Bainbridge to raise the skysails and unreel the main. We're going in now, but I don't want to get there too fast."

It was a nice problem in sailing, to keep in motion and enter the harbor, with its infestation of reefs and shallows, and at the same time to stall their arrival until after darkness fell. Whether or not he could manage it would determine the success of his effort.

16

The *Intrepid*, straining against her sea anchors, gave the appearance of a slow and sloppily sailed craft making a leisurely way into harbor. Above decks a watcher would see a man at the wheel, and half a dozen others all dressed in the same loose sailor's costume, and if they moved with more alacrity than the usual Mediterranean merchant sailors, it was unlikely to bring much notice ashore.

Below, in the hold, which was the only compartment below decks where the men could be assembled and stand up, Decatur was going through a detailed review of their assignments.

"Mr. Bainbridge?"

The lieutenant stepped forward and spoke with such intensity that Decatur was suddenly conscious of Bainbridge's relationship to the captain of the *Philadelphia*, and how much this night must mean to him personally.

"Walker, Parton, McGeorge, Hale, Smart, Martin, and I have the mainmast. We board from this vessel amidships, to port, and make our way to the station, fighting if need be. Each man has cutlass, pistol, and dagger. Walker and

Parton each have kegs of powder. McGeorge has one bundle of oil-soaked rags. Smart has the pitch. Martin carries the fire kit. At our station Walker and Parton run the powder around the mast, and into the stowage lockers, port, starboard, and amidships. McGeorge ties his rags up the lower mast and along the yard as far as he can reach — no further. Our object is to destroy mast and sails. Smart coats the mast with pitch. Smart and Hale stand guard then while Martin fires the lot. Hale and I are guards. If trouble comes we fight our way out and back to the *Intrepid.* If the *Intrepid* is lost we come out by boat to the ketch in the harbor or to the *Siren.*"

Decatur interposed.

"And if the boats are gone?"

"Then we swim. To Syracuse if necessary."

The men broke forth in a cheer, and Decatur knew he had their hearts as well as their hands.

Around the circle he went, and each officer responded in the same brisk way, while the men standing behind showed in their faces that they knew their tasks and were confident. When it was over, an hour later, Decatur searched his mind but could find nothing to add to what had been planned. They had made it as complete as man could do. Their fate now rested in the hands of the gods.

The quiet of dusk began to descend on Tripoli harbor. As the *Intrepid* tacked back and forth across the narrow entrance, Decatur saw before him the two forts, the tall castle, and occasionally he could see a portion of the *Philadelphia*. She was headed up into the incoming tide. Her yards appeared to be fully clothed; the intelligence was all correct, she could make sail and be out of harbor in an hour.

Dusk descended before he could catch a good look at her decks to see how many men they might have to contend with in battle. His observations were interrupted by Pilot Catalano, who came up in the last moments of light to point to the western shore, and the surf still running there.

"That is bad news, signor," said the pilot. "I had hoped that we would have clear passage in, but now we must take the eastern channel. Many more reefs." He grimaced.

"You can make it?"

"I can make it, but like everyone, I wanted it the easy way. Now it will be hard. Your men must be very brisk and sharp when the orders come."

Decatur passed the word that they were entering the channel, and that the men on deck must be alert. The last caution was hardly necessary, for he could sense the tension among the deck crew, and when he stuck his head below, he saw from the instant hailing of his officers that they, too, were waiting eagerly for action.

The night was clear. The offshore breeze brought smells of land, foreign, undefinable smells. The moon came up, the crescent gave enough light to outline the minaret and the masts of the *Philadelphia*, standing like sticks against the bulk of the castle.

Suddenly, peering out behind the headland, Decatur saw a sail, and as the vessel turned, he recognized the silhouette as that of the *Siren*. She had come at last, and was following them in. He watched. She anchored, and a boat pulled away from her side. Good old Stewart. He was constrained to remain on the edge of the action, but he was sending someone.

Oars muffled, the *Siren*'s boat moved surely and quietly through the water, coming up alongside the slowly sailing ketch with her sea anchors dragging behind. Eager hands threw out the Jacob's ladder, and others caught lines fore and aft to bring the boat fast alongside. First aboard the ship was the boat's commander.

"Lieutenant Caldwell at your orders," said the officer, to Decatur, as he snapped him a salute.

"What are your orders, sir?"

"I am to place myself under your command. Lieutenant Stewart sends his compliments and best wishes for your speedy success."

So the plan changed a little, made all the better for Stewart's timely assistance. Decatur's one problem had been what to do about the enemy aboard the *Philadelphia* once the fighting began. Some would leap overboard; some might try to get away in boats. And it was important that they not be allowed to rouse the harbor before the men of the *Intrepid* had completed their work.

Caldwell and his boat full of men, then, would have the task of circling the *Philadelphia* as the *Intrepid* moved up and the boarding began. He would stop all boats from going ashore, and he would pick up or sink every swimmer.

The *Siren*'s boat was pulled aft and towed, to arouse no suspicion, and the ketch continued to move in toward the city of Tripoli. As darkness settled, around seven o'clock, they were inside the reef. Slowly they moved in toward the *Philadelphia*. After an hour, when they were several hundred yards from the ship, Decatur gave a signal, and the men of his command began slipping up from the hold, to throw themselves flat on the deck of the ketch, below the rail and the bulwarks. Another hour passed, with half a dozen sailors moving back and forth along the deck, insouciantly, as though they were on the most innocent of business.

Decatur and Catalano stood aft, by the wheel, and watched every movement in the harbor. They saw a small boat put out from the shore by the castle, heading for a pair of gunboats anchored two cable lengths from the *Philadelphia*. Decatur's heart was in his throat — had someone somehow warned the Bashaw of their coming, and of the deadly nature of their mission? But the boat contained a single messenger, and he went from one boat to another — perhaps delivering orders or mail. His demeanor, and that of his boat crew, suggested that he had not a care in the world.

Darkness had brought a silence to the city. A few lamps and candles burned in the windows of houses that could be seen from the port, and in the castle. But all was still. Even the water was scarcely riffled by the light breeze that stirred the sails of the *Intrepid* so slowly that it seemed they would be all night just getting in that few hundred more yards.

They were so near their destination, and yet so far. Decatur searched the *Philadelphia* with his eyes. There was no sign of life on deck, but that did not mean the ship was not alive with Berber sailors, scimitars drawn, perhaps lying beneath the bulwarks of the frigate, just as Decatur's men were lying low aboard the ketch. What if the spy had been caught, and had confessed everything?

But a block creaked, and the sails of the *Intrepid* flapped as Catalano brought her about a little to fetch up to the port quarter of the ship. The ploy was to be to appear so clumsy as to miss the landing, and sail on by the bow, heading seaward, and then to bump up on the windward side of the frigate as the worst lubber might do. In the confusion the men would move aboard quickly, sheltered by the decks of the frigate from view of the castle.

All went well, Catalano executed a most wonderful lubberly tack, sails flapping and in irons for a full thirty seconds, and then she began to slide in on the starboard side of the frigate.

Just then came a loud, unfriendly hail from the ship.

"Stop! Fend off there! Who are you and where do you think you are going?"

17

The pilot looked at Decatur for orders.

"Tell them we are traders from Malta, and that we were nearly dismasted in this last storm. We have lost our anchor. We are sick, and tired, and half drowned, and now we want to tie up to the frigate during the night."

Catalano put this message into Arabic. From the frigate came a pregnant silence, as an officer was brought to consider the problem.

"What are you carrying?"

"Olive oil from Sicily, some olives, some wine."

"Is the wine any good?"

"By the light of Allah, it is forbidden."

"Come now, let us not be theological. Answer my question."

"It is the best Sicilian wine."

"Ah, that sounds quite good."

"In the morning, when there is light, I would gladly break out a cask for you."

"Even better."

"It is done then, we can come and tie up?"

"A few more questions. What ship is it?"

"The *Transfer*."

"Yes. I know you. The Bashaw has just bought that vessel from the Maltese trader. Why did you not say so?"

"You have given me no chance."

"Why have you been so long in passage?"

"The storm."

All this time, Decatur was itching to move, and his men were ready. The *Intrepid* was edging up to the frigate.

"Stand off there. Are you sure you know how to sail? That last tack was as poor as any I have ever seen."

"Our ship is stove and half full of water, effendi. No one could sail her better."

"Perhaps — but look out there, you're coming in on us."

The *Intrepid* was indeed edging in toward the starboard bow of the *Philadelphia*, but now, just as the Tripolitanian officer spoke, the wind died altogether, and she lay, becalmed, twenty yards off the frigate.

My God, thought Decatur, looking up. For they were directly beneath the loaded guns of the ship, and if there was the slightest suspicion of their true nature, they could be blown out of the water in a moment.

"What was that ketch you were speaking to outside?" asked the Tripolitanian officer.

Catalano translated swiftly to Decatur.

"Be careful," whispered Decatur. "He probably knows Martini. Feel him out."

"That was an acquaintance of many years. A

captain Martini. You know him?"

"Well, and unfavorably. He has aroused the ire of the Bashaw on several occasions. We tolerate him here only because of certain trading connections."

"He means smuggling," whispered Catalano. "Martini is notorious for his opium smuggling."

"I do not know him well, effendi," said Catalano in his most conciliatory manner. "But he hailed us, and I believed he was a subject of the great Bashaw."

"Far from that, Maltese," said the lieutenant. "You can keep better company in the service of your head."

"Your warning is appreciated."

Decatur looked approvingly at the pilot. "Keep on stalling him," he said. "We've got to do something to get in there now. Tell him we are sending a boat with a line."

Catalano hailed the frigate again.

"Effendi, we are becalmed, so close and yet so far. Let us send a boat to the big ship."

"Send your boat, we will meet you halfway."

Catalano pretended to give Decatur an order. The latter held his hand up in front of his face, bobbing in a manner which he hoped would pass for a Berber salute, and moved off to round up the gang of brigands he had parading on deck in their loose costumes. They moved aft to the *Siren*'s boat, brought it in, untied the painter, and began rowing with a mooring line toward the *Philadelphia*.

"Not a sound out of any of you," whispered Decatur. "Let Catalano do the talking."

They brought the line almost to the frigate's side, where they were met by a boat filled with Berber sailors. They took the line and knotted it to one of their own. Decatur, leaning forward to pass the line, was so close to one sailor in the other boat that he could smell the strong odor of mutton fat on breath. He grunted something unintelligible, and moved back and the other sailor moved away without a word.

"Oh, thank you, effendi," came Catalano's profuse expressions of gratitude from above them. "You have saved us much woe and in the morning we shall honor you as you deserve."

"See that it is so," said the other officer, "and make it early so the whole port does not observe what you are at."

Decatur, heart in mouth, was bringing his men back alongside the ketch. So far so good. They had managed to achieve the means of contact. But what next?

On deck, Decatur conferred with Catalano. The Tripolitanian officer answered his question from the other ship, even as he was asking it.

"Mind you," came the word from the tall deck of the frigate, "you are to keep this mooring only until the tide changes. We do not want your musty little boat rubbing the paint off our new warship."

Decatur looked down. Indeed, he had not noticed that in the last few minutes, as he was moving about, the tide had begun to ebb. This meant the lines would hold the *Intrepid* to the mooring with the frigate, but at arm's length, always under those fearsome guns. Something must be done, and quick.

"Get your sails down," came the order from the frigate. "Don't you lubbers know anything at all?"

Here was their chance — the very slight breeze had begun again, hardly more than a whisper, but it could be made to serve.

Decatur moved to the bulwarks, and spoke quietly to Lawrence who was lying there, cramped, waiting as he had been for two hours.

"Get the men to begin pulling, very, very slowly, on that mooring line. We must come alongside."

Lawrence began crawling, taking a half dozen sailors with him, and they moved forward to the mooring bitts. They grasped the line, and slowly drew it taut, while Catalano made a great display of cursing and shouting at the men on deck to bring down the main, and stow the skysails, drop the jib — all the while Decatur telling them to foul the rigging in every way so the sails would not come down properly.

The line tautened, the bulwarks of the *Intrepid* gave such a creak that Decatur feared the enemy officer would immediately guess what he was about. But there was no sound from the frigate, none at all. They were twenty yards off. Then, foot by foot, the men hauled, and the *Intrepid* straightened her bow, in the outgoing tide, to bring her head on into the *Philadelphia.* Fifteen yards, ten yards, then five yards separated the ships.

"Bring that line amidships," whispered Decatur, and Lawrence and his men hastened, crawling down the starboard bulwarks, pulling the *Intrepid* so that her bow moved to face the stern of the frigate, and her starboard beam was drifting into the bigger ship.

Suddenly there was a commotion aboard the frigate.

"What . . ." came the shouted words.

They were just a yard from the ship.

A horn blew, a cutlass rang on steel.

"Americanos! Americanos!" came the cry, and the sound of running feet on the wooden decks above them.

"Come on men. Board her!" shouted Decatur, and he leaped up to be the first to land on the deck of the captured frigate.

18

Stephen Decatur was on his feet on the deck of the *Philadelphia* — the first American to board her since her capture. Midshipman Morris, cutlass in hand, scrambled up next, and jumped onto the deck. On the deck too, now, was Midshipman Laws, whose pistol had caught for a moment in one of the frigate's gunports. Then came the surge of men along the starboard side, each squad of them heading purposefully to a destination, lugging the kegs of powder and the twists of pitch and the oil-soaked rags that would be their tools of destruction.

They were aboard, cutlasses flashing, shouting the watchword *"Philadelphia"* before the astonished Berber sailors could gain their wits, and then there seemed to be so many Americans swarming over the side of their ship that they were overwhelmed.

Decatur had given strict orders that no firearms were to be used unless absolutely necessary, and not a gun was heard. Thus the town was not aroused by this first sign of conflict, for the clang of steel on steel was not unusual. Decatur and his men made the spar deck and cleared it. A few of the enemy stood and fought, but were quickly killed. Others began throwing themselves over the side, to swim for shore, not knowing of the circling presence of Lieutenant Caldwell and his men, standing in their boat, cutlasses in hand, to offer capture or death to the swimmers.

From the beginning, Decatur had determined to hold the spar deck himself with the help of Midshipmen Izard and Rowe and fourteen men. They held it now. An officer came up from the gun deck, aft, and forward, leading a band of men. They were ready to fight, and Decatur lost no time in engaging them. He leaped across the deck, circled the windlass, and was upon them, followed by six of his men. The officer, mustaches that seemed to be as long as his scimitar, paused to do battle, slashing with the sword, so well made for the purpose. But the cutlass was both a slashing and a thrusting instrument, though shorter.

Decatur jabbed at the officer's eyes, parrying to drive the other back. The other Americans found opponents and engaged them, with cutlass, knife and club, and the deck around Decatur was a mass of struggling men, some of them locked together.

The officer, half a head taller than Decatur, had the advantage of reach and the length of his weapon, but he had perhaps feasted too well on the Bashaw's generosity. He was not as quick as the American. The clang of steel rang out again and again, as Decatur parried and turned away the powerful slashes of his enemy. Decatur's arm grew tired, one heavy blow had fallen on the cutlass at the haft, making his fingers tingle and causing him nearly to lose the weapon.

Seeing this, the Berber charged in for the killing blow. Decatur backed, his foot caught in a coil of rope beneath the mizzenmast, and he slid off to one side, the slash missing him by half a foot, and the cutlass caroming off the stout deck. The Berber was after him with passion, dagger drawn, arms wide, moving in like a boxer, ready to strike with either weapon before Decatur could regain his footing. But Decatur dodged around the mizzenmast, regained his balance, and as the enraged Saracen hurled himself around to port, Decatur was ready for the thrust. He parried again, feinted, and skewered his man just below the breastbone, the cutlass grating hard as it struck the spine.

The Berber's eyes rolled, his scimitar clanged on the deck, and he fell lifeless into Decatur's arms, almost immobilizing him just as a second enemy fighter saw what had happened and charged in with a horrible cry to wreak vengeance.

Decatur thrust the bloody corpse from him — against the blow of the new enemy — danced back, and slashed with his cutlass. The other's weapon fell from his hand. He began to attack with poniard alone, thought better of it, then rushed to the rail and leaped over the side, leaving Decatur panting beneath the mizzen.

Looking around, Decatur saw that his men were carrying the day. Izard and one enemy were still sparring on the starboard rail, but the Berber's position was hopeless, for Rowe stood by, cutlass raised, ready to deal a death blow at the first opening. The enemy saw this, and he too leaped from the ship. The other Americans were all on their feet, checking bodies, and dropping the dead over the side. Decatur counted noses, all fourteen men were there — not a one had sustained a serious wound.

Below, Decatur could hear the clash of arms on the gun deck, where his men were fighting with the hard-bitten gunners who had been brought to the ship to take her out to sea. He hesitated, longing to charge down into the battle, but he knew that he must follow his own orders — to hold the spar deck at all costs against reinforcements and any attempt by the Berbers to take the ship to sea.

Aft, Catalano and his party, led by Midshipman Davis of the *Constitution*, had secured the steering, and Catalano cautiously made his way forward to consult with Decatur.

"You know, signor, we could sail her out of here," he said tentatively.

Decatur looked up at the masts. The main and mizzen were sound. The foremast, which had been chopped down by Bainbridge in an attempt to lighten the ship and move her off the reef before capture, was still jury-rigged, but it

166

would carry light sail.

The standing rigging was intact, the running rigging, though refashioned to suit the style of the Berbers, was workable. There was plenty of sail, and Decatur's seventy officers and men could man her easily. Yes, she could be taken out.

For a moment he was greatly tempted. What a coup it would be, to bring the *Philadelphia* triumphantly back into Syracuse harbor, to parade before the astonished eyes of the squadron. Even Preble, who would roar like a lion at the defiance of his orders, could not but be pleased.

But orders were orders. Decatur knew well enough that the commodore was not at all sure he would come back. He knew now that the situation was in hand; the burning of the *Philadelphia* was in progress; his men were already lighting the fires. To stop it all, to attempt to run the gauntlet of the gunboats, would be to tempt fate, and if he failed, and if the *Philadelphia* were retaken, the blow to the morale of the squadron would be nearly irremediable.

He looked pointedly around the harbor. There the gunboats lay, some twenty of them, and Catalano, following his gaze, could see the signs of stirring there and on the shore. The castle was aroused at last. A swimmer had made it through Caldwell's blockade, and the word was ashore that the Americanos had captured the *Philadelphia*. Lights flickered in the upper regions of the castle, and far away the English fort also lighted up.

"We had best be about our business," said Decatur. "They" — he indicated the gunboats — "will not be long."

Down below, Lawrence, Laws, and Macdonough were scurrying along the berth deck, three decks under. Lawrence led the defense party, cutting down three Berbers before the others fled forward and upward to escape the ship. Izard and Rowe cut off some of them above, but most escaped. Below, Laws and Macdonough supervised the placement of the combustibles along the berth deck and in the storerooms. A trail of powder, pitch in the right spot next to a bulkhead, then on to the next compartment.

Above Decatur waited impatiently, until Lawrence popped his head up to announce that all was secure and he was ready to set the blazes. Aft, Bainbridge and Davis now led ten men into the deserted wardroom and the steerage, where they placed their charges. All was ready there.

Midshipman Morris stormed into the cockpit and after storerooms, fighting his way against two Berbers who sought to block their passage until they realized they were overpowered, and fled. Then those compartments were made ready.

Decatur hesitated, it was not yet too late to reverse his decision and take the *Philadelphia* out to sea. But the wisdom of Preble's orders was now borne out by events. Ashore the stirring had become a full cry. Drums were banging, and horns sounding, to bring the Bashaw's men to action. Small boats were quivering in the moonlight on the bank, as their oarsmen prepared them for battle. The gunboats were alive with men, waiting only for some cogent order to bring them into action. To burn her was one thing, to try to sail out, losing the time and waiting for wind, would be to demand a fight in the harbor, and if it was won, then to have to fight the ship out all the way to sea against the combined shot and shell of the forts, castle, and gunboats.

Late as it was growing, Decatur still hesitated. Morris was not yet on deck. He had been the last to secure his gunpowder and pitch. Finally he struggled back to the spar deck, smelling of smoke.

"She's finished, sir," he grinned. "Ready to go."

Decatur sniffed. "She's already ablaze, it seems." His orders had been for the men to hold their matches until told.

"When I got down below, the wardroom was already on fire," said the midshipman. "We had to move fast through there, so I didn't wait either, but told the men to let her go. I hope I did all right."

Decatur smiled and patted the midshipman on the shoulder. "You did just fine, Morris," he said. There, that had ended the debate that raged within him as to whether he should chance a run out. Some eager seaman's match had solved the problem.

On the spar deck now the crackling of flames drowned out the cries of the Bashaw's men ashore, as their officer rallied them for an effort. The smoke, gray and acrid, drifted across the deck, and the flames from aft hid the English fort from view. Then flame shot out from the ports of the gundeck, and amidships. Decatur stood stolidly beneath the mizzen, hearing the report of every detail, and dismissing the men to reboard the *Intrepid*. Only when the last detail had reported, did he speak up.

"All right, boys," he said to his two midshipmen and the sailors. "It's time to go. We've done the job."

And as he swung down into the ratlines of the *Intrepid*, even as the ketch moved away from the side of the burning ship, he could see indeed how well they had worked. Flames were shooting mast-high aft. The mizzen was aflame, and the mainmast, and the yards were burning. The gunports were spouting fire, and even as they pulled away, the guns began going off.

A frightening explosion resounded almost in Decatur's ear, before he had made his way aft to his deck.

"Double shotted," he muttered to Catalano. Just as he had suspected, the ship was manned by real sailors, and was going to put to sea. They had not come a moment too soon.

The guns of the starboard side of the *Philadelphia* menaced the *Intrepid* all the way out, but luckily the fires got to them and fired them over the ketch and around her, and not one shot struck home. But the guns of the port side of the ship sent panic into the ranks of the sailors and soldiers massing beneath the castle, for they began firing with devilish intent into the town itself, and along the beach. Two shots thudded into the battlements of the castle, and tore away a five-foot section of wall. Men screamed and ran to escape the dervishes firing the guns against them. The gunboats, ready to move, received no orders, for the boats that would have taken them were suddenly deserted, as the defenders huddled behind protection from the weapons of the blazing ship.

The *Philadelphia* made her own majestic funeral pyre. The flames licked out and up above the topmasts. She burned with a will, and as the fire found her powder, she began to explode and send fireworks into the air. The poop blew off, and the rudder was thrown high into the air to splash into the harbor.

The *Intrepid* was in deadly danger. Her decks were still loaded with gunpowder kegs and barrels of pitch, and a brand from the frigate or an unlucky shot from one of her guns could blow all of them sky-high. And as they tried to move away from the ship, more danger threatened. The fire doused the wind, and created a vortex of its own. Catalano was first to notice it.

"Signor," he shouted in great anxiety. "Lieutenant Decatur! I am losing way." The Maltese pointed at the sail, and forward. Decatur looked across at the French fort, it was not drawing abaft the foremast as it should. They were standing still, and the sail was twitching like a live animal, as the conflicting air currents played against it.

"We are going back, signor," said the pilot. "The *Philadelphia* wants us to join her."

"Break out the boats," Decatur shouted, and Lawrence hurried to obey. "Get them down and let's begin pulling, boys, or we'll never get out of here," said Decatur as he moved forward to encourage the men.

The *Siren*'s boat was still with them. Lieutenant Caldwell took a cable, and his men began to row the sweeps, pulling hard. Nothing happened. They seemed hardly able to stay the pull of the fire behind. Then Laws in the *Intrepid*'s first boat moved out to starboard of Caldwell with another cable, and Decatur thought he sensed the pull. Macdonough was next with a boat, to port, and the sensation was real, they were pulling away from the burning frigate.

The shore batteries opened up as the ketch moved out into clear view, or as clear as the view could be in the smoke and flames of the burning *Philadelphia* behind. But the fine gunners had been commandeered from the fleet for the *Philadelphia*, and those who were still alive were scattered along the shore cringing among the Bashaw's soldiers against the shot and shell from the guns they had loaded themselves. The firing from the forts was wide, and long, and the firing from the gunboats was scattered, and not one shell even pierced the canvas of the ketch.

Out they went, slowly under tow, until they passed beyond the clutch of the *Philadelphia*'s fire. In twenty minutes they were at the harbor's mouth, the tide helping them out, and the wind fair for Sicily.

Martini and his ketch had quite disappeared, but Decatur felt sure he would see the big smuggler again somewhere.

Stewart had sent out two boats to help with the tow, but they were no longer necessary. And Lieutenant Bainbridge, who had been charged with the task of wetting down the combustibles and powder on deck, and keeping fire away, now could stop sweating and pacing back and forth along the length of his area of responsibility. The danger of explosion was past.

As they crossed the reef line, into deep water, Decatur looked back at the city. The *Philadelphia* was a red and yellow glow against the blackness of the town, sending little showers of her essence upward and out. The cables burned through, and she began to drift in the eddies of the inner harbor, back upon the castle itself. From the port entrance, Decatur and his men could hear the cries ashore, as the burning frigate drifted down on them. And then, even as they watched, the fire reached the main powder magazines, and the *Philadelphia* blew up. Masts and yards leaped into the air, burning sticks thrown high above the city to fall gracefully into the water. A huge ball of flame erupted amidships and shot into the sky, to fall upon the town. As the remnants dropped, the concussion reached the ketch, and Decatur could feel the hot breeze of it even as the sound nearly deafened him. He could imagine how it had affected those on shore, only a few yards from the burning vessel.

She burned red and low then, what was left of her, and after a few moments, Decatur turned his attention away from the wreckage, and out to sea.

"Head her up for Syracuse," he said to Pilot Catalano. "We've a report to make to the commodore."

19

Lieutenant Stephen Decatur did not know it, but as he relaxed on the deck of the ketch, drinking in the clean sea air and watching the sails draw handsomely, he had succeeded far beyond the dreams of Commodore Preble.

The Old Man had been exceedingly raspy in the past ten days, particularly after learning of the storm that swept the central Mediterranean. He did not know if his ships had been lost at sea, or driven ashore on a Berber beach to be captured, so that he would have still another set of men to ransom. He did not expect many of the men of the *Intrepid* to return. Quite possibly they would be burned in the harbor with the *Philadelphia*, if they ever got that far, the commodore growled in the privacy of his cabin.

So he was unprepared, as was the rest of the squadron, for the return of the *Siren* and the *Intrepid*.

As the ships sailed for their base, Decatur pieced together the story of his men's fight, for he had seen very little of it from the deck of the frigate. Anderson had done his job exceedingly well; not until they halted on the first day out and Decatur traveled to the *Siren*, did he learn that the lieutenant had encountered a boat from the *Philadelphia* laden with armed men ready to fight, and had slugged it out with them, sinking the frigate's boat, without losing a man. Indeed, Decatur had not lost a man at all on the whole adventure. Smith's wound was healing nicely; and the only man injured in the fighting was the Quaker, Stone, who had kept himself directly behind Decatur in the fracas on the spar deck, and saved his commander from a nasty blow by fighting off a huge bearded Berber for ten minutes. He had suffered a sword cut on the upper right arm, but in the end he had slain the Berber, and in very un-Quakerlike manner, had pushed the body over the side. Surgeon Heerman looked over both Smith and Stone and told Decatur happily that they would require only minimal medical attention.

So they came home, on a fine February day, sailing into Syracuse harbor, all canvas aloft, with the same saucy impertinence that they had gone out with. Preble should have reprimanded them both, Stewart and Decatur, but as the ships came in and he saw they were sound, he hesitated. Then within the hour Decatur was piped aboard, and entered the cabin.

"Well!" grunted the commodore. It was an exclamation more than a question.

"We burned her to the water, sir," said Decatur. Then he described in detail the explosion that had sent the mainmast of the *Philadel-*

phia turning like a burning windmill high above the ship.

Preble was impressed in spite of himself, and he covered his approval with another brusque question.

"And how many men did you lose?"

"Not a man, sir," said Decatur, and he described the fighting, and the injury to Seaman Smith. His praise of the young Quaker, Seaman Stone, led him further.

"The crew, sir, they behaved like real fighting men. Not a slacker in the crowd. And they went at the Turks with both hands."

"Glad to hear it," grunted Preble, for in recent weeks he had been dogged again by desertions from the *Constitution* and other vessels, part of them at least, occasioned by British promises, and some British threats. It was good news indeed that American sailors still knew how to fight.

So Decatur finished his report, and the commodore softened enough to tell him he had done a good job, before he was dismissed to write it up for the Secretary of the Navy. But Decatur had no sooner left the cabin, than Preble pulled a sheet of paper to him, and began to write.

"Dear Mr. Secretary:

"I wish to inform you of a most unusual and heroic exploit by one of my trusted young lieutenants . . ."

As Preble so wrote, Decatur was making his way back to the *Enterprise*, to resume command and get back into the routine of naval life. It seemed strange, having now to doff the ragged garments in which he had lived for two weeks. But his men knew what he needed better than he knew himself, and when he found his cabin, the ship's tub had been set inside, filled with steaming soapy water. Suddenly he realized how grimy and louse-ridden he had become, and he stripped and plunged into the bath, scrubbing every inch of him, from his toenails to the top of his head, and luxuriating in the comforting warmth of the water.

He turned over the report in his mind. Every one of the officers deserved promotion as recognition of their heroism. As for himself, the adventure had been enough. He was content to have command of the *Enterprise* and such a fine body of men. Now, to avoid the boredom of long days at sea, he had to find another adventure.

As he shaved and dressed, Decatur's mind slowly came back to the world he had left behind him. It was Wednesday again, the day of the Marchesa's weekly soiree. Should he go?

A shadow crossed his face as he considered, for it might mean an encounter with Rosmore. That he could stomach, but it might also mean an encounter with Teressa, and that he was not sure he could manage just yet.

But as he dressed, and put on his hat, he heard the scuffling noises outside his cabin that meant a boat was pulling alongside. Perhaps it was Stewart, so he went on deck to look. But no, it was a harbor boat, and the boatman simply handed a sailor a note, and went away, saluting grandly and smiling.

The sailor brought the message on deck and handed it to Decatur. The handwriting was Teressa's. Not willing to face his men in his embarrassment, Decatur went below to read the message in the privacy of his cabin.

"You were so right," the message read. "I have learned that Rosmore provoked you and intended to kill you. He came to me, lying, the day after you sailed, and I sent him away. Now, just an hour ago, I have heard of your glorious exploit, and I want to congratulate you. You are the bravest and most honorable man I have ever known. Can you forgive me?"

Decatur's heart leaped. Now he whistled as he went on deck, and he was ready to call Bosun's Mate Tyler with the gig, when he spied Stewart's boat coming in from the *Siren*.

Absently, it seemed, he leaned over the rail, heavy headpiece behind him.

"You're undressed, sir," said Stewart from below. "Is that the way they keep the *Enterprise*?"

Decatur grinned. "Where are you bound?"

"To the Marchesa's, of course. To tell her that all the heroic exploits they will attribute to you really belong to me. Come along?"

"I just think I will," said Decatur, clapping his hat on his head and turning it to a rakish angle, as he moved to get into the boat. He was grinning and light of step, for Lieutenant Stephen Decatur was heading for what promised to be a marvelous homecoming.

20

The night was warm and the stars welcoming as Decatur and his friend strode up the cobbled street, heels clapping on the stones with a noise to which Decatur was now quite unused. A few days at sea and one almost forgot how noisy life on land could be.

The street musicians were out, with their hurdy-gurdies and violins, and a pair of urchins halted them to beg a coin, for the Americans were known for their generosity. At the palazzo, the major domo smiled in recognition of the two young officers and beckoned to a footman to take their cloaks and swords.

Decatur took the wide stairs on the marble staircase two at a time and paused at the top, searching the grand salon for sight of Teressa.

There she was, over in the corner, as always, surrounded by a little knot of admiring officers and men in the various dress clothes of Sicilian officialdom. She caught his eye and looked at him in frightened anticipation. Stewart saw an acquaintance, clapped Decatur on the back, and parted from him in the crowd as Stephen headed toward Teressa's corner.

As he approached, a tall figure detached itself from the knot and made its way toward him. It was Lieutenant Rosmore of the Royal Navy, his disfigured right hand clad in a gray suede glove. As Rosmore approached, scowling, Decatur could see the hand flexing. The man was obviously having a difficult time controlling himself.

"We meet again, Lieutenant," said the British officer coldly, standing directly in his path.

Decatur stopped. To have proceeded would have caused him to bump the other, and he supposed Rosmore was again looking for a fight. To step around would be to avoid the other, which simply would have delayed the issue. It must be met. At some point they must confront one another, and although Decatur could see Teressa's hand go to her mouth and her eyes widen, there was nothing to be done about the time or the place. It was of Rosmore's choosing.

"How is your hand?" Decatur asked pointedly.

The other scowled and put it behind him. "I have learned to shoot very well with my left," he said, "and I have always used a sword in either."

"I did not mean that," said Decatur evenly. "I only hope your wound healed satisfactorily."

"No thanks to you, sir," said the tall man. "I shall always believe you intended to maim me."

"Believe what you will, sir," said Decatur. "You will recall the cause of your quarrel with me?"

"Yes. I see you have succeeded in poisoning her mind against me, too. You and your *ex-*

ploits!" Rosmore spat out the word as though cursing.

Decatur said nothing, waiting. The other obviously had some reason for the encounter.

"I have been ordered back to England," said Rosmore, "but I did not want you to think I had forgotten you. We shall meet again." He tapped his gloved hand with the other. "And it will be a different story, I promise you."

"I am at your service," said Decatur quietly. "Any time. Any place." He bowed, and brushed by the Englishman, composing his face in a smile as he turned toward Teressa. She had forgotten the conversation she was in and was staring, white-faced, at Decatur and the departing Rosmore.

As Decatur came up, she grasped him by both hands. "I am so proud of you," she said, "but so worried, too. What did he say?"

"Only that he was returning to England," lied Decatur. Or at least he felt it was a lie, although the threat had really all been implied. But, he reasoned, there was no reason to upset her with it.

"I am so relieved!" she exclaimed. "He has been speaking of you so harshly that I was afraid he was going to challenge you again."

"Nothing like it," said Decatur lightly. "Now tell me, how is your daughter. And your mother-in-law?"

"My daughter is wonderful. She now knows the difference between an American and an Englishman," she replied blushing. "I taught her. And as for my mother-in-law, you know very well you do not care a bit how she might be. But she is fine, too."

They laughed, and only then did Teressa realize that she had not released his hands. She blushed again, quickly pulling her hand away.

"Must you stay here all evening?" he asked.

"Not at all. I came, really, because I hoped you might have received my note. We saw your ships coming in today."

"I am very grateful for it — and very touched."

"I was insufferable to you."

"You were concerned."

"Let us forget it all," she said. "It was all a dreadful dream, and we must talk of other things. I have not much time, again I am the mother and must go home."

"Let me pay my respects to the commodore and my host," said Decatur, "and then may I see you home?"

"I was hoping you would," she answered. "Caterina knows you are home, and she would like to see you."

Decatur was not at all certain that the baby had any such ideas, but he went across to the refreshment table, where he spotted the marchese talking to Preble. The nobleman said good evening, and both men nodded, but they were so deep in discussion of the latest movement of Napoleon that they paid him scant heed. It was a marvelous turn of events, and Decatur strode rapidly back to Teressa.

"Let us get out of here before the commodore realizes that I am ashore," he said. He grasped her by the elbow and firmly ushered her to the stairs. In a moment they had their garments and were in the street.

"A man of action, as they all say," laughed Teressa as they walked together in the street.

"You don't know. If the commodore had taken it into his head to talk, I would have been there half the night."

They walked slowly and companionably in silence to the town house, where her servant opened the door and escorted Decatur to the drawing room. He waited while she ran up the stairs to see Caterina and prepare her, looking around the room. It was the same and as friendly as ever. He now felt a little part of it and at the same time felt the tug of his conscience. For where could this lead? How could he, merely a lieutenant in the United States Navy, aspire to the affections and even consider marriage to a woman of such culture and means? It was ridiculous on the face of it. Yet all he had to do was find his coat and step out into the street and the problem would be solved. So, he told himself, he was a liar and he knew it. And he did aspire to affection, and perhaps even a more permanent relationship with this lovely young countess. There was no reason she couldn't come to Philadelphia and become a citizeness. He laughed at the term; it would never become so proud a beauty.

In ten minutes she was down, dressed in a different gown, and laughing she took him up the stairs. Little Caterina looked at him, popped her thumb into her mouth, gurgled, and began to giggle. She buried her head in her mother's ample bosom and would not emerge.

Teressa took her in her arms, cuddled her, and put her to bed, then arm in arm she and Decatur moved back down the marble stairway to the cozy library, where a discreet footman had prepared a fire, brought wine, and withdrawn before they entered the room.

They sat together on the broad divan, one of the type that reminded Decatur of the Moorish influences here in Sicily, and she poured wine for him. They talked. She insisted on a complete account of the adventure, and he gave it without boasting. She grew rapt as he told the story of the actual burning of the ship, and her face colored as she seemed to share the sense of excitement. When he had finished, she pulled him toward her.

"Oh my dear," she said, "you might so easily have been killed — and I could not bear to lose you now."

He sought her lips, and soon there was silence in the room.

Well before morning Decatur was back in his cabin aboard *Enterprise*. When Preble's boat came early in the morning, as he had known it would, he was ready with his report and dressed

186

in his best uniform for the interview with the Old Man. Silently the boat pulled for the flagship. Decatur went aboard to salute the colors and then was escorted by a marine sergeant to the commodore's cabin. The sentry saluted as he passed the door, and the Old Man, sitting at his desk, as usual, looked up. He actually smiled.

"Well, Decatur," he said, "it was a good job and you did it well. I must say I'm still surprised that you didn't lose any men."

"No more than I, sir," said Decatur. "Every one of them was a hero, and every one of them deserves a promotion."

"I wish I could give it," said the commodore. "But you know Congress and economy."

It was true. Congress had stripped the navy entirely after the revolution and was only now beginning to recognize the needs that must be met if American commerce were to succeed in competition with that of England and France. But among those in Washington were many who dragged their feet, and thus getting promotions and awards was never easy.

"What I can do," said the commodore, "is let it be known in the men's records that they participated in this action. It will count for them when they go to other ships, and they will get their promotions, one way or another."

"Thank you, sir," said Decatur.

"And what about yourself?" asked the commodore.

"I want nothing," Decatur answered. "It was

an honor to be assigned the task, and I am pleased that we did it well. The glory, sir, is quite enough for me."

"Well said!" the commodore exclaimed. "I agree with you. A man makes his reputation as he can, and the rest takes care of itself. You certainly have caused a stir here. MacClellan is here in the *Warsprite*, you know, and he told me last night that Nelson is going to hear of this. You'll be famous, my boy, in every drawing room on the Continent and in England."

"I would rather be famous in Philadelphia," Decatur remarked with a smile.

"Well," said Preble with a wry smile, "I rather think you will be." For he was recalling the letter of the day before, now entrusted to one of the ships sailing for America, in which he had asked the Secretary of the Navy to promote Decatur and give him whatever honors Congress would bestow. "But right now I did not call you here to chew over the cabbage we ate yesterday. I have a new job for you if you want it. If not, then Stewart . . ."

"Yes, sir," Decatur interrupted, "I am sure I will like the assignment."

"Wait until you hear what it is, young man," growled Preble. "Then you might not like it so much. You know the Bashaw — well, he has friends at court, and they are intriguing, I am quite certain, to draw the Two Sicilies into the struggle and embarrass the United States. If you take this job, you'll be spending part of your time at court and part of it at sea."

Decatur grinned. The night before, Teressa had told him tearfully that she had been appointed lady-in-waiting to the queen for the next six months and that she could not refuse the honor. That meant that she would leave for the court and would be spending the weeks in the winter palace and in the summer estates, far from Syracuse. Now Preble was holding out the promise that Decatur could spend at least some of those weeks with her. The offer was like a golden sword.

Preble looked him over shrewdly. "That little countess seems to appeal to you quite a bit, doesn't she? She's a nice girl, and you could do much worse. Don't you go breaking her heart, young man, or you'll have me to answer to."

Decatur looked at him very seriously. "She means too much to me, sir, to have me cause her a moment's indisposition."

The commodore coughed loudly and blew his nose to wipe away this lapse into frivolity.

"By the way," he remarked, "I'm putting you in command of the schooner squadron. That's part of the job. I can't give you any more money or a promotion, but at least you can be lieutenant-commander."

"Why thank you, sir! But do you believe I deserve the honor?"

"If I didn't think so, I wouldn't give it to you, son," said Preble crustily. "Now go on back to your ship and wait for orders. You haven't forgotten how to do that, have you?"

Decatur looked blank.

"Mr. Dent told me how you took *Intrepid* out of here, breaking every rule in the book." His eyes twinkled. "If you hadn't come back with the story you had to tell, believe you me, somebody would have gotten unshirted Hell."

Decatur grinned an imp's grin. "Yes, sir," he said, saluting. "I await orders, sir."

He strode out of the cabin, stepping high and quickly, stopping at the rail to look out over the American fleet. Four schooners and a handful of gunboats — that was to be his command now, and even if he was still just a lieutenant, that put him up alongside Dent, at least in the structure here in the squadron. It was very satisfactory. Now all he had to do was earn those honors — and in a way that would please Teressa.

A bosun came to the rail and piped him over the side, and he realized that all the squadron knew, too.